URBAN LEGENDS

THREE NEW TALES OF TERROR

LEIGH KENNY, DAN FRANKLIN, AND NICK ROBERTS

Book 20 in Crystal Lake's Dark Tide series

Let the world know:
#IGotMyCLPBook!

Crystal Lake Publishing
www.CrystalLakePub.com

WELCOME
TO ANOTHER

CRYSTAL LAKE PUBLISHING
CREATION

Join today at www.crystallakepub.com & www.patreon.com/CLP

HAVE YOU HEARD ABOUT THESE URBAN LEGENDS?

ADAM CESARE

"**H**AVE YOU HEARD about these clown sightings?" Someone asks me in 2016. "Clowns threatening people with knives and machetes, in random cities?"

And I respond. . .

Look, I don't remember how I actually responded. But I'm sure I said something polite.

People at parties, non-horror people at non-horror people friends and family gatherings, I'm always polite and enthusiastic, when they make the effort to bring up a topic they think will interest me, 'the horror guy.'

What I likely said was along the lines of "cool!" or "wow that's creepy" or "there's video? Where'd you see it?"

But—I'll confess now, almost a decade later:

I was being polite and nothing more.

I couldn't have cared less.

I did not find the rash of "clown sightings" gripping America cool or creepy.

They felt lame, contrived.

Because in my jaded heart it was some Reddit thing. Something for the clicks. An urban legend that wasn't. More a viral challenge that wasn't *really* scary or menacing or organic. For all we knew then, it could have been a promotional stunt for a Cartoon Network show or an edgy soft drink. It was probably an idea that originated in a marketing firm, that would only end when someone was fired.

And I thought like this because—even way back in 2016—we'd sucked the fun out of the internet. Or the internet had sucked the wonderment out of us. Or me. Whichever way the sucking went.

Which sounds—what? Ungrateful?

But this is a foreword to a book and the only rule in forewords is that you have to be 100% honest.

And it does make me feel ungrateful.

Because those clown sightings planted the seed, became a zeitgeist-y thing that snowballed into a book series that is. . .my main source of income. Those folks in dime-store masks with their purposely graining photos/videos started a domino effect to allowed me, a guy who initially shrugged them off, to put food on the table.

"Have you heard about the man who lives behind Brian's house?" Someone asks me in 1998.

"What?"

"You know how Brian's house backs up to Heckscher Park? There's a guy that lives back there. He eats cats and dogs."

No. I had not heard about that. But Brian's my best friend. I sleep over his house all the time. Our friends often play manhunt out in that backyard, the yard where there's not even a fence dividing it from the woods.

And the idea that there's a man living back there, killing and eating suburban pets, *terrifies* me.

So what's the difference here? Why did one of these two "Have you heard about. . ." stories work on me while the other didn't?

Well, sure, I'm 10 years old in the second example.

And that's part of it.

But that's not the whole of it, either. So let's not focus on me, still wearing OshKosh.

The man who lived behind Brian's house didn't make any sense. Brian's mom called the cops if a skateboarder so much as looked at her curb. Brian had a dog. The dog was very much alive and uneaten.

And I knew all that.

I was a smart kid.

Consciously, I knew there wasn't a man living behind Brian's house.

But there's also part of the story I *wanted* to believe.

Because doesn't that make those sleepovers that much more

exciting? Add a sense of adventure (and mortal danger) to any future games of manhunt?

Urban legends aren't about credulity or incredulity, credibility and the incredible. They're a magic mix of how you're told the story and what you want out of it.

I don't care if it's a man with a hook for a hand on Lover's Lane, that one house on your block where satanists live, the gang initiations that leave you bleeding by the side of the road, one ear poorer, or even the Lara Croft nude code.

These myths work because we—either through fear or hormones—*want* to believe them. When we believe the unbelievable, we're in control of the chaos.

Which, now I could be talking about the horror genre in general, fiction and film. It's why I love this stuff, why I've dedicated my life to it.

Because the stories don't always work for me. Sometimes it's the storyteller's fault. Sometimes it's just my mood, that I don't want to believe, can't find my fear dial, get it tuned just right.

But for these three novellas you'll want to believe.

And you won't, at the same time.

Kenny, Franklin, and Roberts know what they're doing.

So pour yourself a cup of tea. Or grab a beer, who am I to judge?

Maybe snuggle into a blanket.

Try not to think about whether you locked the door.

I'm sure you did.

Probably.

Read on, but before you do that: indulge me.

I've got to say "take two!" to 2016.

Okay.

I'm back at that party.

I'm in the right headspace now.

I want to believe you, so. . .

Tell me again.

What's up with these clown sightings?

KNOCK ON WOOD

LEIGH KENNY

IT'S COMING

THE ONLY THING that stood out about that Tuesday was how well the rain held off for that time of year. By morning, most of the Abbott family would be dead or disappeared, but for now, all was as it should be in the creaky, old house on Hawthorne Avenue.

On the far side of town, hidden among the forested hills that overlooked the small town of Creedence, all was not as it should be.

The Rayner Jones State Hospital stood proud and timeless in every dull shade imaginable, unseen by most but for the slate-grey apex that poked above the tree line. The people of Creedence knew it was there—heck, a good portion of them either had worked within its dreary walls in some capacity at some point in their lives, or still did—but they chose to disregard the hulking building, glad that the state had elected to build it outside of town.

Where both the building and its occupants could be mostly ignored.

Most of those who called Rayner Jones home were harmless; people whose families had more money than maternal instinct and chose to farm out the care of their relatives to others, or people who just temporarily cracked a little deeper, a little more visibly than was societally acceptable beneath the pressures of life. The most secure wing of the building, however, had long been used to house those who perpetrated real harm. Some set fires. Some caused damage to things that weren't theirs. Some were turned on by things that shouldn't arouse them.

And some were killers.

Dennis Stanley sat on his off-white bed sheets in his off-white state-issued hospital pajamas. The small room around him was not off-white, but still off in its own way. The scant pieces of furniture in the room—a metal-framed bed, a wooden closet, and a folding chair with a faded floral cushion on its seat—sat on scuffed linoleum the color of sour milk. The one window in the room was a small square of reinforced glass that sat halfway up the metal door. A pale face pressed against the glass, watching Dennis as he rocked on the off-white sheets upon the metal bed. His small, wiry frame was pulled tight as he muttered to himself.

Jess pulled her face from the small window and turned to the other orderly. "What do you think he's saying?"

"Fucked if I know," Mel replied, stifling a yawn. "Are we going for a smoke or what? If we don't go soon, it'll be almost time to clock off. I need a cigarette before then."

Jess nodded, but still her eyes returned to the man swaying on the bed.

Dennis had been a resident in Rayner Jones for almost twenty years now, and she had never heard the man utter a single word in her four years on the job. Others who worked there longer said the man spent his first few days in hysterics, begging the staff to listen to him. To believe him.

He didn't do it. He didn't kill his family.

After those first days, they put him in a room on his own; this room with the bed and the chair and the cupboard. Every second he spent not in a drug-induced state of comatose, he screamed at the closet. It was always the same thing he wailed over and over.

"Mister Upside Down."

The orderlies were advised to no longer knock before entering his room. The sound would send the man into hysterics. Most complied. Some continued to do so on occasion, just to see the abject fear that would temporarily replace the usual blank slate of Dennis Stanley's face.

Eventually, he stopped screaming.

He barely uttered a sound now, barely lifted his eyes from the floor most of the time.

Watching him rocking back and forth, his eyes wild and white, Jess felt the first stirrings of unease gnawing at her gut.

"Should we get someone? This isn't normal."

Mel scoffed. "Nobody in here is normal. There's nothing normal about murdering your wife and kid. Nothing normal about not even having the decency to tell the police where their bodies are." She tipped her head towards Dennis's room. "And in case you hadn't noticed, Jess, we *are* the someone's around here."

KNOCK ON WOOD

Mel was born and bred in Creedence. Would likely die within its confines too. She was under no illusions, had no grand plan of escape. She knew the stories about the tragedy that unfolded within the walls of the Stanley's home on Hawthorne Avenue. Knew the whispers and urban legends that spawned from that awful night. Her own mama kept the younger version of Mel in line with threats of summoning Mister Upside Down. Everyone knew the boogeyman wasn't some creature that crawled from the closet at night, though. At least, the residents of Creedence did. The boogeyman around these parts was all too real, and the only thing that separated her from him now was a locked door.

"We'll check on him really quick and then have a smoke break. Aren't you curious about what he's saying?" said Jess, fumbling in her pocket for her keycard. Behind her, Mel rolled her eyes in resignation as the other girl swiped the lock. The mechanism clicked and the door opened with a hiss.

The orderlies entered slowly and quietly. Dennis continued to mutter and sway.

"Dennis? Mr. Stanley, is everything okay?"

Still, he swayed and muttered, paying no mind to the pair of women in his room.

Mel sighed heavily, annoyed at Jess, annoyed at the man who was keeping her from her cigarette, and annoyed at herself for not being able to quit the damn cancer sticks. "Mr. Stanley!" she barked, rapping her knuckles against the metal surface.

Knock-knock.

Dennis froze.

He screeched, jumping to his feet and rushing towards the women.

Gasping, Mel stared into his wild eyes. His bony fingers grasped at her tunic. She could feel Jess's feeble attempts to pull him away but couldn't bring herself to do the same. Frozen, she stood nose to nose with the killer and listened to his muttered whispers.

"It's coming. Don't you hear the knocking? He wants to get in. It's coming. It's coming. He's coming!"

Dennis's body slumped, as though someone had unplugged him or flipped an invisible switch. He shuffled back to the metal-framed bed and lay on his side on the off-white sheets, his bloodshot eyes focusing on the wardrobe in the corner.

Jess pulled Mel from the room and slammed the door. The lock clicked back into place and both women looked at each other uneasily.

"Let's go. We've earned our smoke after that!" Jess said, breaking the silence that started to stretch taut between them. "Shift will be over soon and he'll be someone else's problem."

The women moved through the hallway and up the stairs almost silently, each lost in their own thoughts. Jess still wondered what the man had been saying. Mel finally started to relax and was thinking about how impressive the story would be when she told people. Nobody cared about what went on within the walls of Rayner Jones until something exciting happened. She grinned to herself as Jess swiped the keycard once more and both women stepped outside onto the balcony.

The view from here was incredible. The space was officially unusable, too dangerous to allow the residents access to, but the cigarette butts strewn around the weed-choked patio stones were a testament to its unofficial use as a smoking area for the staff of Rayner Jones.

Mel pulled a cigarette from the box and perched it between her lips as she delved into the pockets of her tunic in search of the lighter. Next to her, Jess bounced on the balls of her feet, trying to stave off the cold with movement.

"Will you hurry up with the lighter," said Jess, her teeth chattering.

"I can't find it," she hissed back, but her words were swallowed by a loud wailing that began to shake the building. Mel and Jess looked at each other in panic.

The fire alarm!

Scrambling through the entryway and back inside the building, the women rushed back down the stairs and through the hallway, the usual squeak of their tennis shoes against the linoleum drowned out by the overbearing trill of the siren. They didn't speak a word to each other, and yet they both knew where they were headed: Dennis Stanley's room.

Mel tried to recall her encounter with him in more detail. She could still feel his hands twisting against the material of her tunic, could still feel the weakened tug as Jess tried to pull the man away. She could see the crimson streaks of lightning that painted his bloodshot eyeballs as he stared into her eyes. Into her soul.

KNOCK ON WOOD

It's coming.

Could Dennis have taken the lighter then? He must have. It was the only explanation for the missing lighter coupled with the sudden onslaught of the alarm.

Skidding to a halt outside the room, Jess swiped at the lock. There was a moment of regret as the acrid smog enveloped them both, stinging their eyes and tearing at their throats with dry, black fingers. Within an instant, the cloud of smoke thinned out as it dispersed into the hallway and continued on its way. Dennis was nowhere to be seen.

Out in the hall, the sounds of shouting and banging were barely discernible above the ringing alarm. Mel knew one of them needed to start unlocking the other rooms. They needed to get the other residents to safety. Other staff members would be here any minute to help. Nobody could willfully ignore the screeching wail of the siren.

But both Mel and Jess stood rooted to the curdled-milk linoleum just inside the room. Through watering eyes, both women stared at the smoke billowing from a crack in the closet door.

The cupboard burst open and Dennis lurched out.

His pajamas were no longer off-white but blackened, charred, and melted into his flesh. Flames sprouted from his head. From everywhere. The skin on his face slopped downwards drastically, melting away like plastic. One eyeball lay deflated in its socket, bubbling and sizzling against the heat that claimed it. The other eye saw everything.

The women screamed.

"He's here! He's here!" shrieked Dennis, his voice no longer his own as his vocal cords shriveled and snapped in the heat. Still, the terror was evident in his tone and in his one functioning eye. The fiery figure collapsed in the middle of the room, and Mel cried out as hands grasped at her from the smoke.

Help had arrived.

As her colleagues led her from the room, choking, spluttering and still screaming, Mel could see the charred remains of Dennis surrounded by crude, ashy scribblings that adorned the walls and the bubbling linoleum around the burning wardrobe. The words made her feel sick, like the floor was tilting. Like something was wrong. Like something was coming. The words scraped along her throat in a whisper.

"Mister Upside Down."

IT'S NOT TRUE

A FEW SHORT miles away, a gaggle of teenagers loitered around the backyard of the house on Hawthorne Avenue.

"I'm just saying, I wouldn't be able to sleep at night in this place," Gabby said as she passed the cigarette along.

Lucas Abbott cocked an eyebrow as he accepted the smoke from his friend. He stuck his head out of the lean-to and surveyed the back of his new home. "Don't be stupid, Gabbs. They're just silly stories," he replied.

The Abbott family had recently purchased the ramshackle house on Hawthorne Avenue and spent a couple of weeks painting and moving furniture, boxes of clothes, and knickknacks from their rental above the butcher shop in the middle of town. Today was their first official day in their new home. Their forever home, as his mom liked to remind him.

Lucas and his parents moved to Creedence almost ten years ago now, and he knew the rumors as well as anyone. He still remembered his first day of school after moving to town. He had listened, wide-eyed, as his new friends Gabby, Erica, and Tony told him about the house on Hawthorne Avenue and of the terrible fate that befell the Stanley family.

Of Mister Upside Down.

Seven-year-old Lucas had been both terrified and enthralled, and a lifelong bond was forged that day among the four kids. Many a summers day throughout their youth was spent cycling past the house, daring each other to open the gate, walk up the weed-choked footpath, or touch the front door with its chipped and peeling paint. Never knock, though.

Nobody ever dared to knock on the door.

They were friends, after all, and none of them wanted to see any actual harm come to their small group.

KNOCK ON WOOD

Rumors always seemed to circulate around the house on Hawthorne Avenue.

The Stanley family massacre.

The Brown family, who moved in a couple of years after Mr. Stanley had been locked away in Rayner Jones on the hill, fled in the middle of the night, stopping only long enough to pin a note to the entrance with instructions for their realtor to sell the place, burn the place, give the place away if they must.

Then there were the stories about different kids over the years.

Karen Larsen, Jim Donohue, Dawn Keate. . .all gone. All last seen around the house on Hawthorne Avenue. Karen and Jim ran away together. Star-crossed lovers, or so everyone said. Dawn ran away alone. Ran all the way to LA, the old ladies of the town said as they exchanged titbits of gossip like currency. No way Mr. and Mrs. Keate would have allowed their daughter to become an actress. No, they wanted her to follow in the family footsteps and eventually take over the butcher shop. But what teenage girl would choose a life of blood and guts over the glitz and glamour of Hollyweird?

Still though, the stories persisted. The legends grew legs and crawled like insects into the nightmares of the children of Creedence. The adults might blame murder and miscreants, but the kids knew better. The boogeyman lived in the house on Hawthorne Avenue.

Ian and Katie Abbott had scrimped and saved until they finally had enough to obtain loan approval. The loan only covered small apartments and barely standing properties that were no good for the couple, their three children, and Boo the cat. The house on Hawthorne Avenue, however, was a steal. It was a little dated and ramshackle, sure, but nothing that some love and the laughter of a family couldn't fix.

Lucas was horrified.

He didn't believe the legends. Not anymore. He was almost seventeen and far too mature for such flights of childish fancy.

But nobody wanted to live in the local murder house. The one that made kids run screaming in the other direction. The one that people whispered about. Being a teenager was already fraught with discomforts. The inability to disappear into the background would seriously cramp his style. Lucas was sure some of his classmates were already working on nicknames inspired by his new address.

Rolling the words around their mouths, trying them out for best size and maximum effect.

But living on Hawthorne Avenue meant living closer to his friends.

Not to mention the lean-to shed at the back of his new home, which seemed like the perfect hangout spot. It was a little dusty from misuse and it was lacking in space since his parents stored most of the original furniture from the house out here, but there was enough room for them to lounge comfortably, and it was sheltered from the weather. Lucas could also keep an effortless watch from the open side of the shed, allowing the friends to smoke cigarettes without parental interference. Maybe they could upgrade to include a few bottles of beer the coming weekend. He knew Tony frequently pilfered alcohol from his dad's stash. Gabby still had some of the vodka leftover from their last camping trip, too. A little housewarming with his friends might be just the thing to settle his nerves.

Through an upstairs window, Lucas could see his little brother's form silhouetted against the light. Smiling, he watched as Alexander zipped around his new bedroom, a toy plane or rocket in hand whooshing through the air.

A tall, thin figure stepped into view and Lucas's stomach dropped as the larger silhouette lifted his little brother into the air and disappeared from sight.

Hiding the glowing tip of the cigarette behind his back, he watched for a moment longer. The bedroom light went out, and his shoulders finally relaxed. His dad would be occupied now with bathing Alexander. His mom was likely already occupied feeding his baby sister, Clara, before bedtime. That constant nagging concern of his parents catching him smoking could be swept aside temporarily. Dragging the smoke deep into his lungs, Lucas coughed a little, exhaled, and turned back towards Gabby and Erica.

Gabby and Erica looked at each other incredulously.

"Are you for real, Luc? Families have gone missing, AND a bunch of kids, and you think it's just "silly stories"? C'mon dude, you're smarter than that," said Erica as she plucked the cigarette from his fingers.

Before he could protest, she offered him a wink. Lucas turned on his heels before either of the girls could see the pink hue that flooded his cheeks. Stupid hormones.

KNOCK ON WOOD

He dragged an old corduroy armchair from one shadowed corner and flopped into it, hoping any remaining color in his cheeks would be blamed on the exertion of moving furniture. "There's a big difference between a guy losing his shit and murdering his wife and kid and blaming a boogeyman for a bunch of coincidental stuff," he said, leaning forward to take the smoldering cigarette from her fingers.

"Not just any boogeyman," whispered Gabby, "Mister Upside Down."

Rolling his eyes, Lucas opened his mouth to speak but his words were drowned out by a loud bang behind him.

Knock-knock.

All three teenagers jumped to their feet. A tiny shriek escaped Erica, and Lucas felt heat rise in his cheeks once more as she pressed against his side, her hand reaching for his.

KNOCK-KNOCK-KNOCK.

The sound was coming from an old closet at the back of the shed.

Lucas watched with wide eyes as the door bounced in its frame with each pounding knock against its surface. The banging continued, a rapid-fire staccato rapping from within the confines of the hulking piece of furniture. Lucas crept closer, slowly reaching out towards the handle. His fingers grazed the wood in the same instant the hammering stilled on the other side. He turned his head and glanced at his friends in confusion, yelling out in surprise as the wardrobe suddenly burst open.

The girls screamed.

Lucas continued to shout as he stumbled away from the closet.

He realized too late that the girls weren't howling with fear, but with amusement. Behind him, Tony fell through the double doors, clutching his sides as tears of mirth streamed down his face.

"I got you so good, Luc," he chuckled.

Looking at the sheer delight on his friends faces, Luc couldn't stay mad. All three of them were clearly pleased with their prank, and his embarrassment and anger subsided, replaced with humor and a shit-eating grin.

"You guys are a bunch of dicks. I should have known you wouldn't be able to help yourselves. Mister Upside Down," he scoffed.

"I still wouldn't joke about it too much," said Gabby, sliding another cigarette from the box. "And I sure as shit wouldn't sleep in that house."

"You can't seriously believe there's a real boogeyman living in this house," Luc replied. He raised his eyebrows and scanned his friends' faces. He didn't want to believe in stupid kiddy stories, and he needed them to confirm their disbelief too.

"I heard he lives in cupboards and stuff."

"I heard he can appear anywhere in the house, so long as there's a door for him to come through. That's why nobody ever knocks around this place, doofus."

Tony looked at Erica with mock hurt. "I knocked on that one, and I'm just fine," he said, nodding his head towards the large piece of furniture. "I don't think the knocking thing is real." He rapped his knuckles against the shiplap walls of the lean-to in demonstration.

"I heard that Dennis Stanley was holding seances and that's how Mister Upside Down got through. You know the superstition thing, to knock on wood? Well, I heard Stanley knew something bad had come through and kept knocking on it for good luck; to try to ward off the thing that was stalking him and his family. But it didn't work."

"So, Mister Upside Down is probably attracted to that sound now. It's like ringing a damn dinner bell!"

Lucas shook his head in disbelief. "Shit, you guys are talking like this thing is real. You're even starting to creep *me* out, and I think it's all bullshit."

Tony, Gabby, and Erica turned to look at him, as though realizing where they were for the first time.

"Sorry Luc, you're right. We shouldn't be talking shit about your new house before you've even had a chance to spend the night." Erica reached out and touched his arm gently.

"True enough," said Tony, stubbing out the cigarette he held and pulling a crumpled packet of gum from his pants pocket. "We'll know for sure soon enough just how real the legends are!"

They all took a stick of the proffered gum and began to say their goodbyes as they strolled to the front of the house together, stopping only to watch as a cherry red fire engine roared along Hawthorne Avenue and right past the house with its siren wailing. It was headed for the hills that overlooked Creedence. Trundling along behind the fire truck came Steve the mailman, headed home after a long day of deliveries. He waved at the teenagers and gestured emphatically towards the tree-covered hillside. A thin plume of dirty grey smoke had begun to curl above the tree line, obscuring the usually visible roof of the Rayner Jones State Hospital.

The four friends stood silently for a moment, watching the trail of smoke rise higher into the darkening sky.

"Guess one of the nutters went nuts again," Tony said casually, prompting the others to burst into laughter. Goodbyes were uttered and promises to text each other if anyone heard what had happened out at the local crazy house.

Lucas trudged up the path, smiling to himself as his friends' voices died away into the evening. The feeling of eyes upon him stopped him in his tracks, and he looked up at the house. He watched it for a moment, and it watched him back. It was just a house. Nothing more. No boogeyman.

As he stepped inside and pulled the door closed behind him, Lucas tried to ignore the rapping that had commenced at some point during the short stroll from the sidewalk to the back of the house. It sounded distant, but not distant enough. It sounded as though it was coming from the lean-to. That same staccato tapping against the wooden closet.

Knock-knock.

IT'S SCARING ME

IAN ABBOTT BRUSHED the hair back from his youngest son's forehead. Alexander's skin felt clammy, a sure sign that he was stressed. With his other hand, Ian glanced at the crumpled sheet of paper. The figure that gazed at him from the lined page made his hair stand on end.

Was it any wonder Alex couldn't sleep?

"Buddy, it's too late to be drawing pictures. And it's never an ideal time to draw creepy pictures. You've scared yourself."

Alexender's huge brown eyes watched from behind the comforter.

His heart tightened, a concoction of pity and love for the small boy. It was cliché, but Ian struggled to cope with his emotions when any of his kids were distressed. He looked back at the crude drawing: the jagged limbs, the scrawl of dark hair, the leering face that was drawn upside down. He shuddered a little, then leaned forward and planted a soft kiss on Alex's cheek. "No more drawing. It's time to sleep, little man."

He stood and stretched, then stuffed the drawing in his jeans pocket. Ian gathered up the scattering of crayons and loose pages that dotted the bed before trailing across the room and depositing them on the small desk in the corner. He cast a critical eye around the space. They would eventually have the third bedroom completed, and then Alex would no longer need to share his space with the baby, but for now, between his sons bed, his daughters crib, and the various tents, toy chests and other small pieces of furniture, Ian decided that tomorrow he and Katie would need to spend some time reorganizing their youngest sons bedroom. Perhaps Lucas would take his little brother to the park to expel some energy while Clara was down for a nap. Then, he and his wife could tackle it as a team.

KNOCK ON WOOD

He could think of better things to spend their child-free time doing, though.

Ian grinned to himself, amused that all these years and three kids later, Katie still had such a powerful effect on him. She was as gorgeous now as the day they met. Even more beautiful when viewed through the lens of a husband and father who worshipped his wife and the family they created together.

His foot snagged on the edge of the pop-up tent, and he stifled a swear, catching himself before he hit the ground. Peeking into the crib, he was relieved to see that Clara hadn't budged an inch despite the combined excitement of her brother's creepy bedtime art adventures and her father's clumsy attempts to maneuver around the cluttered space. With a gentle, practiced hand, Ian lifted the blanket higher, beaming as his tiny daughter shifted and nuzzled against his palm. How lucky could one man be?

"Daddy?"

Ian turned to Alexander who lay perfectly still beneath his own comforter. Only his eyes were visible through the small viewing window he created in the nest of blankets. If he hadn't spoken, Ian would have assumed the boy had already drifted off to sleep.

"Daddy, will you check the closet before you go?"

None of his kids had asked him to check for monsters before. Not under beds. Not in wardrobes. Ian was sure that when he searched on Google later, some childhood expert would reassure him that the move was causing his son to experience some temporary distress. *All perfectly normal*, they would tell him from behind the screen, from a video recorded sometime in the past when perhaps things were perfectly normal. It hurt a little now to see Alex struggling, and despite the house being a good thing for them all, he understood too how disarming it would be for a child. A new house, new bedroom, new sounds to become accustomed to. Like that knocking sound, for instance.

And as his ears adjusted, Ian realized that the sound was coming from the closet area.

No wonder Alex wanted him to check for monsters.

Poor kid had probably lain in bed, working himself up over what was likely to be something completely innocent. Best case scenario, it ended up being something Ian could fix.

Fix the weird noises, fix his sons fear.

"Sure thing, buddy," he replied, glancing once more at Clara whose tiny rosebud lips quivered as she snored gently. Moving across the room, Ian was careful to avoid the tent this time. As the gentle tapping continued, his mind flicked through the Filofax of information he stored over the years as his subconscious attempted to fix the nameless problem. *Mice, loose connection, rotting wood...*

As he reached out to grasp the handle, the sound stopped.

Behind him, Alexander whimpered.

The soft rustling of blankets informed Ian that if he were to turn around now, his son's large chocolate eyes would no longer be visible through the mound of blankets. The poor kid was terrified, and the weight of his fear was almost contagious.

Swallowing heavily, Ian opened the closet.

IT'S IN MY HEAD NOW

LUCAS CLIMBED THE darkened staircase, reminding himself to add lightbulbs to the list his dad pinned to the refrigerator. The landing wasn't much better, the only illumination coming from the weak beams of moonlight that pierced the curtainless window at the top of the stairs. The rest of the space was enveloped in gloom, the silhouette of each bedroom entrance a dreary grey against the blackness. Beneath his own door further down the hall, a faint strip of light was visible, and his fluttering pulse settled just a little, comforted by the pale glow.

A quick shower and then he'd retire for the night. Tomorrow would likely be another busy day. His dad needed his help a lot to get the place in shape since Mom was busy with Alexander and Clara, but it made him feel good to be needed. Sure, he spent most of his free time with his friends and generally preferred their company to that of his parents, but it still filled him with warmth to know his dad trusted him to do things properly.

Lucas knew that in this day and age he was lucky to have such a stable home life. It seemed like every other kid in his class had an absent parent, an alcoholic parent, or crappy siblings they didn't see eye to eye with. One girl in his class was removed from the school just last year after landing herself in the hospital for the fifth time in as many months. She tried to take her life—one lacerated wrist at a time—and after the final attempt, social services finally became involved. It turned out the girl had been used and abused since childhood by her father and uncle. Lucas felt his heart constrict at the thought of what his classmate endured. Not for the first time, he counted himself lucky that his parents were both so cool. His mom was one of the kindest souls he knew and his dad was fun and dependable. Neither were perfect, but to Lucas, they were damn close.

Something in the shadows reached out, brushing against one of his bare feet. It pulled Lucas from his reverie in an instant. He hissed, his heart rate spiking once more as he frantically scanned the dark hallway.

Boo, the family cat, mewed and twisted her furry body around his ankles, drawing a chuckle from him.

"Christ, Boo. You scared the shit out of me," Lucas said with a grin. He reached down and scratched the cat behind the ears. Her body rumbled like an idling car as she purred and nuzzled against his hand.

Knock-knock.

Lucas straightened suddenly, startling Boo who yowled in annoyance and darted away. The shadows swallowed the cat whole.

Knock-knock-knock.

With a gulp, Lucas turned towards the tapping sound.

It was coming from Alexander's bedroom.

Before he could react, the door swung open and Lucas cried out.

"Sshhh!"

His dad stepped from the room quickly, pulling the door behind him. It closed with a soft click.

"You scared me, Dad!" Lucas held a hand to his chest, his heart thudding against his ribcage. Against his trembling fingers.

Ian studied his son for a moment.

"That seems to be catching around here," he said finally, his face softening. "Your brother was a little scared tonight. I think the new surroundings are getting to him. Check out his drawing. Super creepy, huh?" Ian pulled the crumpled drawing from his pocket and passed it to Lucas. "You know he asked me to check his closet for the monster. Not *a* monster. . .*the* monster."

The paper shook in Lucas's grasp as he gazed at the horrifying apparition his little brother had drawn. It was a crudely drawn man, but its face was the wrong way around. The childish rendering was chilling in its simplicity, and Lucas had to drag his eyes from the page.

"The monster?" he asked, hating how his voice broke. He felt like a small child again.

His dad chuckled as he took the drawing back from Lucas. "Yea. Mister Upside Down, he called it. Funnily enough, I did hear a tapping sound in the cupboard. Didn't see anything though. I'll add it to the list for tomorrow. It'll be easier to check for problems in the daylight. You okay, Luc?"

Lucas forced a smile and nodded his head.

"Yeah, just tired is all. I'm gonna grab a shower and hit the hay."

Ian watched him for a beat before clapping him on the shoulder and heading towards the stairs.

"No worries, son. Just keep it down. Don't want to frighten your brother any further. Oh, would you mind taking Alex out for a bit tomorrow? Maybe to the park or something? It'll give your mom and me a chance to get some organizing done."

"Sure thing, Dad. Goodnight."

Lucas stood and listened as his dad's footsteps disappeared down the stairs, then pushed open the bathroom door and flicked on the light. The naked bulb blazed overhead, and Lucas wondered idly if his dad added one of those globe covering things to the list. He made a mental note to add it himself in the morning if it wasn't already listed on the scrap of paper that clung to the fridge, as light as a feather but heavy with the weight of a thousand small tasks.

The bathroom was small, just a toilet, a sink, and an enamel tub with a shower unit attached. Directly opposite the pedestal sink, a small wooden doorway was set into the wall; a built-in closet that housed the families towels and wash cloths on one shelf, their lotions and potions on the other. Lucas eyed the opening nervously then chided himself for being absurd. His friends' stupid stories had gotten under his skin, coupled with Alexander's creepy drawing. The fact that Alex called his monster Mister Upside Down was purely coincidental. He could have overheard someone else. He could already be on the receiving end of the local Creedence legends and lore. Lucas was about his age when he first heard the stories. It would make sense that the kids in Alex's class would be falling over themselves to tell his little brother about the sordid history of their house on Hawthorne Avenue. About Mister Upside Down. He pulled open the cupboard, grabbed a towel, and let the door close. He turned towards the bathtub and twisted the faucet, wincing as he recalled his promise to his dad that he'd keep the noise to a minimum.

Knock-knock.

Lucas froze.

Before he could turn towards the door, a flurry of knocks and taps sounded. Water spurted from the tap.

The pipes. Of course it was the pipes. The old house was likely going through its own readjustment period after lying empty for so long.

Lucas felt like an idiot for allowing himself to be pulled along by silly stories about a stupid boogeyman. He grinned as he pushed the lever that redirected the water, and laughed aloud at the knocking that followed before the steaming water began to cascade from the showerhead above. Lucas stepped out of his clothes and into the tub, pulling the curtain across the rail, a thin but somewhat effective barrier between his bare skin and the cold air that circulated in the small room.

Tomorrow he would take Alex to the park. He would make sure his little brother knew that there was nothing to fear. Maybe he'd round up the gang too, and they could treat Alex to an hour in the new arcade that recently opened on the other side of town. That would give his mom and dad some time together too. Things had been hectic. They deserved to spend some time in each other's company without worrying about their offspring. Well, at least two of their offspring. Lucas drew the line at taking care of Clara for extended periods. She was a very well-behaved baby, and he never minded helping his mom out by giving the tiny girl a bottle or reading her stories, but changing dirty diapers was not something Lucas wanted to do. No, Clara would be staying behind tomorrow, but one kid was surely easier than three.

A shadow fell across the thin shower curtain.

"I'm in here!" called Lucas, his cheeks flaming as he prepared to cover his dignity from whoever had entered the room.

He was sure he'd locked the door behind him, though.

Knock-knock.

Lucas stilled.

The water continued to patter against the enamel tub. The suds rolled from his body in fluffy clumps and circled the drain before disappearing forever, taking the sweat and grime from his body with it. His heart raced. The shadow moved closer.

His eyes never left the shower curtain as he reached behind him to twist the knob. The water cut out with a gentle hiss.

He held his breath and stood still.

The shadow, a murky stain against the frosted-white material of the curtain, stayed still, too.

KNOCK ON WOOD

Without allowing himself to think too hard about his actions, Lucas reached out a shaking hand and dragged the curtain open, snapping the plastic material from some of the rings in his haste to see what was watching him from the other side of the thin veil.

Nobody was there.

The space that had just been occupied by the looming shadow was empty. There was nobody in the bathroom but Lucas.

He stepped from the tub and wrapped the fluffy towel around his waist, eyeing the broken plastic rings that studded the linoleum floor.

He'd have to add curtain rings to his dad's list too.

Embarrassed at himself once more, he stalked across to the mirror above the sink and rubbed the condensation from its surface. Over his shoulder he could see the small closet. It was open a crack. It hadn't been knocking he heard after all. Just the old door clicking open.

Lucas brushed his teeth, his eyes straying to the mirrored image of the storage space behind him. Bending forward, he spat foamy water from his mouth, then straightened. His eyes sought out the closet again.

This time, the door stood open.

His eyes wide, Lucas scanned the reverse image, his eyes roving over the darkened interior until they landed upon the nightmare figure. The leering face—upside down just like in his brother's drawing—grinned at him with a too-wide smile. Startled, he spun around to face the creature.

The storage space was closed up tight, the darkness and all it contained held back by the flimsy piece of wood.

Lucas twisted his head to the mirror again, but the reverse image matched what he just saw. It was still shut, and Mister Upside Down was still just a figment of his imagination, conjured up by an overactive, overwrought and overtired mind.

He needed sleep.

Down the hall, he dried and dressed in his bedroom as quickly and as quietly as he could. Despite himself, Lucas found his eyes straying to the closet in his own bedroom.

Did they really need so many storage areas in the house?

He turned out the light and snuggled into his bed, relieved at the wave of tiredness that washed over him. Sleep would come easily.

But still he lay there. His eyes were drawn continually to the wardrobe, his mind seeing that horrible figure each time he closed his eyes. Sleep continued to evade him in favor of waking nightmares.

Finally, feeling defeated and pretty annoyed with himself, Lucas dragged his exhausted body from the warm confines of his bed and flicked the overhead bulb on. Bright light burned, the savior of every scared child, lighting up every inch of his bedroom.

Satisfied, Lucas crawled back into bed and pulled the covers over his head.

Safe.

IT'S GOING TO BE OKAY

PULLING KATIE CLOSER, Ian nuzzled her neck and growled theatrically. Her body shook against his as she giggled quietly.

"Mr. Abbott," she whispered, her faux-stern tone cracking as his fingers brushed against her skin. "How could you possibly be ready for round two?"

Ian kissed her neck and ceased the exploration of her body as Katie yawned. Her hinged jaw cracked, and Ian snorted.

"Guess we aren't all young and spritely," he teased.

He knew by the mumbled response and the slow and steady rhythm of her breathing that Katie would be asleep in seconds. Hell, she deserved it after the performance she put on tonight. Ian grinned at the memory, allowing sleep to wash over him too.

Shhhhhhh.

The soft sound slowly penetrated the veil of sleep that spun its web around Ian. He lifted one eyelid, but nothing seemed amiss.

The room was still dark.

The sound had not followed him from his sleep.

Next to him, Katie snored softly. He pulled her close, absently pressing his lips to her bare shoulder before sliding beneath the waves of slumber once more.

SHHHHHHH.

Both eyes sprang open, instantly alert to the small square of light projected onto the ceiling from the handheld video baby monitor on the bedside locker. Ian reached for the small contraption, his heart hammering in his chest as the same sound flowed from the tinny little speaker.

Shhhhh.

Someone was shushing his kids.

Sitting upright in bed, his feet preparing to hit the ground running, Ian gazed at the black and white screen through bleary, sleep-veined eyes.

The kids were asleep, and the room was otherwise empty.

Holding the small device to his ear, Ian could hear the gentle murmur of static. Could that have been what he heard? That was if he even heard something to begin with. Feeling sheepish, he remembered his conversation with Alex earlier that night. How could he expect a small boy not to be creeped out by the new sounds in their house if he was guilty of it himself?

On the screen, Clara's small body rolled over then stilled again. He heard her small snort and sigh and glanced with a smile at his sleeping wife who shared the same habits as their infant daughter. His eyes moved across the screen, past the open closet, past the small play tent in the middle of the room, finally landing on the small lumpy form of his young son, asleep in his own bed.

Satisfied that all was well, Ian placed the monitor back on his locker, nudging it away from the edge, then turned over and pulled his wife close once more.

He was asleep before the screen timed out on the monitor.

IT'S JUST BEGINNING

ACROSS THE HALL, Alexander watched in horror from the safety of his blanket nest as the nightmarish figure stepped from the open closet.

IT'S ONLY A DREAM

IN THE BEDROOM at the far end of the hallway, Lucas tossed and turned as the day's strange events seeped from his subconscious into his nightmares.

Knock-knock.

In his dreams, something hammered on the other side of his wardrobe, but when he flung it open, the banging would begin over his shoulder on his bedroom door. Then his windows. Then his walls.

Incessant knocking.

A cacophony of bangs and clatters as something fought to gain entry. Until suddenly, all the sounds stopped in unison, followed by a simple *taptaptap* from within the closet once more. Lucas reached out to open it, his mind screaming at his arm to stay by his side, his fingers not to wrap around the handle and pull, but before he could resist whatever forces pulled his strings like a marionette of skin and bone, the door creaked open, and his friend Erica stepped out.

A calm washed over dream Lucas.

Everything would be okay. It was only Erica.

Unease crawled along his spine and prickled his scalp as he watched her tiptoe across the carpet towards him, but still he smiled at her.

She smiled back from a face turned upside down.

IT'S GOT HER!

MISTER UPSIDE DOWN leered at Alexander from across the room.

With a whimper, the small boy ducked beneath the covers. If he couldn't see the monster, it couldn't hurt him.

Right?

The floor creaked. Silence followed.

Then another creak.

Closer this time.

Alex squeezed his eyes as tightly as his bladder ached, threatening release. He shivered within his flimsy sanctuary of blankets.

Across the room, Clara began to grumble and fuss.

The floor creaked again, but this time the sound was moving away from him and towards his baby sister.

Shhhh.

A tiny gasp escaped him as he listened to the monster soothe his sister. In an act of outward bravery that he didn't quite feel on the inside, Alex pulled the blanket back enough to uncover one eye and forced his eyelid to open.

The monster was nowhere to be seen.

Mister Upside Down was gone.

But no, he wasn't, Alex realized as the quiver of the curtains caught his eye.

A shape was just distinguishable against the thin material and when Mister Upside Down's head suddenly popped out from behind the drapes, Alex felt his bladder finally let go. Warmth flooded his lower half and almost instantly turned to a chill. The boy couldn't take his eyes off the monstrous face that was wrong in ways his young mind couldn't begin to comprehend.

As though pleased with the response it elicited from the boy, the figure turned its attention back to the tiny girl in the crib.

Tears coursed down Alexanders cheeks as Mister Upside Down bent forward and lifted his sister into the air. The creature sniffed the infant, a black tendril of tongue licking thin lips that rested upon the top of its head and leaving a glistening trail of slime in its wake. Its mouth unhinged in an instant and Clara's head disappeared into its depths, the beginnings of a shrill cry from the girl cut off with a sickening crack.

Alexander shrieked his sister's name, instantly regretting the action as the monster lunged towards him. It hissed at the child, an awful sound filled with the screams of the dead and dying, then bolted back towards the wardrobe faster than it had any right to. As the door closed behind what was left of his sister and the monster who took her, Alexander opened his mouth and screamed.

IT'S NOT WHAT YOU THINK

THE BABY MONITOR screen lit up in tandem with the shrill cry that escaped the small device, and Ian jolted from his slumber, eyes still screwed shut against the piercing LED screen. He fumbled blindly around the surface of his bedside locker. His fingers touched cool plastic and he opened one bleary eye just as the screen went dark again. Another cry belted from the speaker, and he winced as he pressed the small button on the side.

Still nothing.

The screen stayed stubbornly dark.

With a sigh, Ian pushed himself upright. He suspected the bulb had blown and now Alexander was likely freaking out in the dark in his strange, new bedroom. What a shitshow their first night was. He sighed, then sucked the frigid air through his teeth as the soles of his feet made contact with the cold floorboards.

Maybe his expectations were too high. Given the urban legends attached to the old house on Hawthorne Avenue, Ian knew deep down that the settling in period was not going to be a smooth one.

As he stood, he pushed the baby monitor across the sheets towards his wife.

"Gonna check on Alex and Clara, babe. After this one though, tag, you're it."

Katie groaned sleepily and reached for the device.

Ian crossed the room and tiptoed across the hall as silently as possible, before realizing that his creeping entry would probably just serve to scare Alex even more.

"Just me, buddy," he whispered, knocking gently against the door.

Knock-knock.

Someone tapped back on the other side, startling Ian.

His heart raced just a little as he pushed it open, a shaft of light from the hallway chasing away a portion of the gloom but calmed as soon as his eyes fell on the sleeping form in his son's bed. He glanced towards the lamp, its usual soft glow replaced by a cold darkness. His eyes returned to his son and he watched Alex for a moment, a smile on his face. Satisfied that the boy was sleeping, he turned towards his daughter's crib, careful not to trip over the play tent. The hallway light didn't penetrate that side of the room, and everything had been swallowed by the shadows. He took another careful step towards Clara.

Something rustled inside the tent.

Ian stood still, straining his ears.

Mice? *Rats?*

Jesus, he hoped not.

The costs just kept adding up in this house. Making a mental note to add traps to the to-do list pinned to the fridge, he dropped quietly to his knees and pushed his head into the tent.

A sea of faces stared back at him.

A dozen black eyes shone in the weakly filtered spear of light and Ian fell back, momentarily startled.

Teddy bears. He was looking at Alexander's collection of stuffed toys. Cursing his own idiocy, he crawled a little further into the tent. Lots of places for a rodent to hide in here among all the small, stuffed bodies. That kid had really created a whole new family with his stuffies. He scanned the furry faces, each one filling his mind with one memory or another. Fluffy Bunny, Marty the Monkey, Rover, Barney, Alexander—

Ian gaped as his son blinked.

The boy's large brown eyes were filled with tears and he held a trembling finger to his lips.

"But. . .How did you get here so fast? You were just. . ."

Alex was fully crying now, his tiny shoulders shaking. "It's in my bed," he wept.

Ian turned his head in horror.

The shape was still in his son's bed.

Someone was in Alex's bed.

He reached out and cupped his son's cheek. Pressing his forehead against the boy's, Ian's heart wrenched as he felt Alex shudder against him.

"We're going to leave the tent very quietly," he said to Alex, his voice less than a whisper. "You are going to run to mine and Mom's room and tell her to call the police. I'm going to get your sister."

"She's gone. He ate Clara."

Ian's stomach dropped as his son's words fell between them like a weighted thing. The air around him seemed to shift all of a sudden and the fear in Alex's eyes was enough to turn his blood cold.

Behind him, a shuffling sound.

Ian turned slowly. . .

IT'S GOING TO HURT

"**D**ADDY!"

Alexander stared in panic at the vacant space his father occupied just a moment ago. Before the monster took him. Disbelief paralyzed him. Mister Upside Down had taken his daddy.

Trembling, Alex pulled his stuffed animals closer. He wanted to bury himself beneath an army of stuffies, so deep that Mister Upside Down would never find him. He could stay there forever and think about all the fun stuff he'd do with Daddy and Mommy and Lucas, even with Clara. If only he could wake up from this scary dream.

Because it must be a scary dream.

There was no way a monster just stepped out of his closet and ate his baby sister and took his big, strong dad away from him. If the monster could defeat Daddy, what hope did Mom have? Or Lucas?

What hope did he have?

He sniffled and squeezed his eyes even tighter.

"Buddy?"

Relief flooded his veins at the sound of his dad's voice and Alex's eyes shot open.

Mister Upside Down looked at him, their faces inches apart.

The monster grinned.

Alex screamed.

IT'S NOT IN YOUR IMAGINATION

KATIE WAS PULLED from a deep and dreamless sleep by the sound of her son's screams. The screams bounced around the walls of her subconscious and followed her into wakefulness like a siren. Beside her, Ian lay unmoving. Nothing more than a shape beneath the covers.

Lifting the baby monitor, she tried to bring the screen to life, but it stayed black. She held the device to hear ear and knew by the soft static sound that the battery hadn't died. The longer she listened to the static that whispered from the monitor, the more her stomach twisted with unease. Her skin crawled as Alex's screams echoed in her mind again. Knowing she needed to check on her children, Katie steeled herself for the cold and glanced at the screen in her hand as it burst into life.

A figure stood in the middle of her children's bedroom, illuminated by the glow of the lamp.

Katie gasped. Her hand flew to her mouth, her fingers trembling as she watched the man. It wasn't a man though. It was a thing. A creature.

A monster.

And it was standing between her children's beds.

It grinned, the hideous mouth at the top of its head peeling downward. Its upside-down face sneered at her. She had no doubt that it knew she was watching. Scrambling from her bed, the cold no longer a concern, Katie couldn't tear her eyes from the screen as she stood at the foot of her bed. Indecision rooted her to the spot. Like a deer caught in the lights of an oncoming truck, she swung from option to option like a pendulum, aware that whatever decision she landed on could mean life or death. She was also aware that this could simply be a nightmare. How could there be a man in her children's bedroom in the middle of the night; a monster no less. That wasn't real life. Monsters didn't exist. She needed to act, or wake up, or. . .something. She needed to do something.

Katie watched as the figure waved, its grin stretching wider and wider to hideous proportions. It began to move backwards, stepping confidently across the floor and backing up into the closet.

Its eyes never left hers for a second.

Long, taloned fingers wrapped around the wooden edge of the opening and the cupboard began to close inch by inch until only a crack remained. And from that splinter of blackness, she knew it continued to watch her. Could *feel* it watching her.

"This isn't real. This isn't real." The mantra repeated beneath her breath, rolling across her mind like a banner on the news channel as she hurried across the hall. She swallowed deep and pushed the bedroom door open, watching the space open up before her. The closet was still open a crack, but her attention was instantly taken by the emptiness of the room. Her babies' beds were empty. No sign of Alex or Clara. Not a sound to be heard of either one. No sound except for a gentle tapping.

Knock-knock.

Katie knew the thing in the wardrobe was messing with her.

She crouched down, reaching beneath Alex's bed for the baseball bat she knew was stuffed beneath it. It was child-sized, but it was wooden and would inflict at least some damage if she wielded it with enough force. Glancing at the empty space that should have been occupied by her youngest son, Katie felt her blood boil and knew force wouldn't be an issue.

A hand wrapped around her wrist.

Startled, she pulled free and watched in horror as the creature's upside-down face leered at her from beneath her son's bed. Scrambling backwards, Katie scooted along the floor until her back hit Clara's crib. She pulled herself to a standing position, jolting as a hand reached from behind and caressed her skin. The small hairs on the back of her neck stood erect as she turned, reluctant to drop her gaze from the monster under the bed but needing to see what fresh terror awaited her.

The creature was behind the curtains now, its arm extended still as its clawed fingers reached for her again. The rest of its frame was hidden poorly behind the thin material of the drapes, and Katie shrieked as its head popped out. It pulled its arm back and covered the eyes on its chin before peeping at her again in an over exaggerated, almost playful manner.

It was messing with her, she knew that. And still, it was horrifying.

Katie pissed herself.

Warm urine ran down her bare leg and pooled on the floor around her feet. In that moment, everything stopped as she wrestled with the very real sensation of wetness. As the glistening trail of urine began to dry to a chill against her skin, the room lurched, and Katie's stomach flipped.

Was it real?

Was all of this real?

Before the thought could sink in, the closet burst open, and the monstrous figure lurched from its shadowed depths and ran at her.

Startled by its speed, Katie allowed her intuition to take over and fled.

Out of the bedroom, across the hall, back to the safety of her own room. She dove into bed and began to shake Ian's sleeping form. Slowly, he turned towards her.

"Ian! Ian, there's something in the children's room! The children are gone, and. . ."

The words died upon her lips as she faced the monster in her bed. It grinned its awful upside-down grin as it pulled her down next to where it lay on her husband's side of the bed.

Just like Ian always did, it pulled her close, but unlike Ian, it wasn't warm and it didn't bring her comfort.

Katie wept as it opened its mouth, wider and wider.

The sounds that came out drowned out her cries.

It sounded like knuckles rapping on wood and the screams of her children.

IT'S TOO LATE

LUCAS JOLTED AWAKE in a panic to something holding him down. He fought whatever constricted him. As the cobwebs of sleep fell away from him, he realized it was nothing more than his bed sheets that bound him, twisted and damp with his sweat.

Erica's upside-down smile flashed in his mind like a neon sign and his breathing became labored and panicked once more as his eyes darted around the dark room. The overhead light no longer blazed and his skin prickled with unease. Snippets of the earlier conversation with his friends seemed to float around the gloomy space, becoming so loud Lucas was no longer sure if what he heard was only in his head.

And then the knocking started.

It chased away all other thoughts and feelings, replacing them with a cold knot of fear that sat heavily in his stomach like a lead weight.

Knock-knock.

Lucas glanced at the closet. There was no question that it was the source of the sound. As though by design, a shaft of moonlight fell through a gap in the curtains, almost perfectly illuminating the closed door.

That was beginning to open.

Inch by inch the gap widened, blacker than the black darkness that shrouded the rest of the bedroom.

"Fuck this," Lucas muttered.

He jumped from the bed and bolted from the room, slamming the door behind him, then wincing at the sound that cracked through the silent house like a gunshot. He stood there for a moment in the dim light of the hallway, his hand gripping the knob for dear life as though he expected someone or something to try and follow him from the room. When the handle didn't budge or jiggle after a few moments, Lucas was almost surprised. Self-doubt crept in and melded with the fear, creating a potent mixture of emotions that left the teenager immobile.

What should he do? Wake Mom and Dad? Sleep on the sofa?

A memory flooded his senses of a time in the not-so-distant past when Lucas—awake way later than he should be playing video games—heard his little brother cry out in fear. He set the controller aside and went to investigate. Alex had been plagued by a bad dream, so Lucas lay next to his brother, promising the young boy that his presence would be enough to keep the nightmares at bay. He had fallen asleep himself, the hypnotic, even breathing of his brother lulling him into a deep and dreamless sleep of his own. He awoke the next morning confused but refreshed to Alexander's smiling face looking at him.

The memory made him smile and he knew in that moment what to do. He'd go to his siblings' room and share his brother's bed.

It was his turn to seek comfort.

As he tiptoed through the hallway, Lucas noticed an almost oppressive silence hanging over the house. Maybe he had grown too used to the constant barrage of background noise when they lived in the apartment before. Still, though, even for the suburbs, Hawthorne Avenue sure was quiet at night.

And now he needed to pee.

Just great.

Diverting to the bathroom, he didn't bother locking the door. It was as silent as a grave around here. If anyone got up, he'd hear them.

Lucas emptied his bladder, wincing again as the stream of urine splashed against the porcelain bowl like an Amazonian waterfall.

Had he always been this loud, or was this a newly acquired skill, he wondered idly as he flushed. The whooshing gurgle of water didn't elicit any guilt this time. He had already made a ton of noise. He hadn't woken them at this point.

His family may as well be dead.

The thought strayed unbidden into his mind and stopped him in his tracks. What a horribly morbid thought.

Lucas turned the faucet from hot to cold.

The rush of freezing water would do nothing to help him return to sleep, but it was an excellent distraction from the sudden snapshots that filled his mind of his family in various stages of death and dying.

Dad with his unseeing eyes, his neck snapped and canted to one side. A single bead of blood hung suspended from his cold, grey lips like a raindrop from a flower petal.

Mom, her face twisted in a silent scream, her eyes, nose, neck, thighs streaked with blood from whatever defiled her inside and out. Lucas began to feel queasy.

Alex filled his mind's eye now, still hanging on in the shadows of a cold, dark place. Every fiber of his tiny body was on fire with pain and terror, so tangible that Lucas was sure he could feel it himself. He scrubbed at his eyes, unaware that tears were tracking along his cheeks. The cold water ran from the faucet to his hands as he stared without really seeing into the mirror that hung over the sink. Over his shoulder, the door to the storage space began to inch open.

Beyond his trembling brother, Lucas could see the tiny, lifeless form of his baby sister. Clara's broken little body resembled that of a doll. Her skin was so pale it was practically porcelain, and she looked almost perfect in her eternal slumber. Perfect if not for the sizeable chunk of her head that was no longer there. One half of her face was ruined. Where her tiny rosebud lips and long lashed eye had once been was now a mash of gore, a canvas of black and red and pink. Despite her no longer being whole, Lucas was sure he could still hear her crying.

Knock-knock.

Shaken from the nightmarish vision, he looked at the mirror's reflection and froze. Every breath he had left was squeezed from his body as his eyes met those of his father.

His mother. His brother. His sister.

There they all stood, crowded together in the shadowy recess of the bathroom cupboard, their eyes opaque but somehow beseeching.

Lucas screamed.

He ran from the bathroom and into his siblings' room.

Both beds were empty.

The tapping began again from within the closet.

Lucas ran, this time across the hall to his parents' room.

KNOCK ON WOOD

The bed was not empty.

A single shape lay covered by the layers of bed sheets his mother always insisted on despite his dad's complaints about it being far too warm. The shape lay unmoving, and Lucas's eyes were drawn first to the small blooms of scarlet that dotted the white sheet, black upon grey in the dim room. Then he noticed the foot that poked out uncovered. One toenail, painted in his mother's signature turquoise blue, stood perpendicular to the surface it was supposed to cover. Blood pooled around the heel drawing his eye to the small, tattooed heart that held the initials of Lucas, Alexander and Clara.

Choking on a sob, he stumbled from the room and towards the stairs where the sound of tiny footsteps seemed to ascend to greet him. Confused, Lucas's ears strained at the familiar sound as his eyes tried to comprehend how he could hear Boo's paws coming up the stairs when the cat hung suspended and slit from neck to tail above the top step.

An eruption of vomit, hot and steaming, spattered on the floor around Lucas, coating his feet in steaming chunks of everything he ate that day. The small footsteps turned to knocking as the house descended into a chaotic cacophony of clatters and bangs. The closet doors opened and closed. The walls and windows clattered and banged.

Lucas dissolved into a mute, shivering mess in the hallway of the creaky, old house on Hawthorne Avenue.

IT'S COMING FOR YOU

LUCAS ABBOTT SAT on his off-white bed sheets in his off-white state-issued hospital pajamas. The small room he found himself in at the Rayner Jones State Hospital was not off-white, but still off in its own way. The only pieces of furniture in the room—a metal-framed bed, a wooden closet, and a folding chair with a tattered cushion on its seat—all sat on scuffed linoleum the color of sour milk. The one window in the room was a small square of reinforced glass that sat halfway up the metal door. A pale face pressed against the glass, watching Lucas as he rocked on the off-white sheets upon the metal bed, his wiry, teenage frame pulled tight as he muttered to himself.

"It's coming. He's coming. . .

". . .IT'S COMING FOR YOU!"

NESTING

DAN FRANKLIN

CHAPTER 1

"**T**HAT'S NOT MY BABY."

The two nurses exchanged a look. The older one reminded Amanda of a dark-skinned Kathy Bates and the other was a suntanned twenty-something with her hair dyed an unnatural red, but their expressions could have been cast from the same mold, carried the same wordless judgment she'd seen on her mother's face for damn near forty years.

She was being *that girl.*

The ultimate condemnation, the summary of the mediocre, the stereotypical, the truly disappointing. To be *that girl* was a fate on par with death. Forget all those teenage nights she spent terrorizing her classmates with stories of hook-handed killers and Bloody Mary, fear of being *that girl* was the childhood memory that haunted her the most. She pawed at her filthy hair, tried to sort it out so she'd look less crazed, but it wasn't much use. Sweat had set into her hair and skin, left her feeling itchy and greasy, her blonde hair in dampish, stringy coils, matted to her face.

"Ma'am—" the younger one began, her voice taking on the kindly, nervous tone people use with strange dogs.

"It's not. You made a mistake. You brought the wrong baby. You have to go find mine, go check again. Check. . .check with the doctor?" She wished her voice held more conviction, but everything seemed muffled and distant and strange. Everything hurt. She tried to summon some air of command, but the well of her willpower was as empty as her belly. The only things left wriggling inside her were the usual scraps of shame and a growing confusion. Panic, she decided. That's what she should be feeling.

Neither of the nurses moved toward the door.

Kathy Bates made a show of checking the chart.

"Doctor A is busy with other patients right now," she admitted, and Amanda hated herself for feeling a flicker of relief.

Dr. A was part of the problem.

Everything was wrong, had been wrong, ever since Bobby had dropped her off at the front doors, a warrior riding off, alone, into battle. The gray-haired nurse made no effort to conceal her impatience as she held up the laminated page as if it were holy text. "This," she gestured to the crib, "is your baby. See the name? Weight? Date? We don't make mistakes like that. Don't believe all the things you see on television."

"No, but. . .you don't understand. You don't—"

She was fifteen again, standing in the center of the living room while her mother gave herself a manicure, Amanda hanging her head in shame after the most recent complaint by one of the other girls' parents. Unable to even meet her mother's eyes, instead studying the woman's nails as she worked.

You let me down, you know that? This is why you don't get invited places. This is why you don't have friends.

Amanda wanted to bring her knees up to give herself something to hide behind, but the hospital cot was punishingly firm, an unyielding prison slab, and the aching throb between her thighs crescendoed into a bellow any time she so much as shifted her hips. She studied the room instead, the faux-oak-paneled walls that were carefully selected to give a feeling of calmness and security. As if she were nested up inside some massive, weirdly plastic tree, all planned and flawlessly arranged. It reminded her of a psych ward.

Amanda wondered if the nurses knew about the weeks she spent in St. Martin's Behavioral Center. She didn't need to see their faces to know that every syllable scurrying out of her mouth radiated pure insanity.

That girl.

And then there was nothing else for her to look at, so she turned to the wood-framed bassinet they'd rolled beside her bed, and the cargo inside.

Looked down at the baby that was not hers.

"It's a common fear," the redheaded nurse offered, and Amanda felt an overpowering desire to nod along, to accept the free pass that said *You're not crazy, you agree. Only crazy people would disagree.* "Lots of people have a hard time feeling that initial bond. You spend so much time with the baby inside you that anything less makes you feel like the baby might not be the same."

Oh, he looked the part. Mostly. Tiny, perfect toes and fingers, a face more or less proportioned the way it should be, his wrinkled skin so soft and gossamer-delicate it looked like it might come apart if she touched him. A pink, bubblegum mouth that chewed on nothing at all, gaped and clenched intermittently as it tested its boundaries and worked out little mewling cries, but it was the mouth itself that caused Amanda's confusion to at last give way to something blacker.

There, sprouting from the tiny gums, front and center, was a tooth.

CHAPTER 2

AMANDA SQUEEZED HER eyes shut for one long moment and tried to sort through the blurry mess of thoughts that were strewn around the wreckage of her mind. She felt like a house that had been broken into, vandalized, graffitied in red. Her memories were slivers of shattered glass, past and present senselessly intermingled, and she picked through them with clumsy, aching fingers.

The birthing plan had fallen apart a few moments after Bobby dropped her off. She'd insisted that she go in alone, fight through it on her own, claim the baby all for herself. It had seemed like such a good idea when Doctor Kate discussed it with her. Doctor Kate was soft-spoken and wide-smiling, her skin tinged with the sprayed-on, unnaturally orange-brown tan that Amanda always associated with poison. She wore a loose t-shirt that had a lotus on it instead of a lab coat, when they first met, and Amanda had no problem imagining her doing yoga.

Doctor Kate was also absent.

In her place, a tiny, rigid-backed knot of a woman, dark scrubs speckled in slightly darker stains. Her eyes were like ink as she peered at Amanda from behind a rigid black plastic mask that swathed her face and swallowed her expression. For a moment, Amanda couldn't help but think of those awful beaked plague masks, and in her distraction, she missed the woman introducing herself.

"Don't bother trying to pronounce it. Just call me Doctor A," the woman said. Her voice was muffled, her accent muddied into something that sounded slightly inhuman.

"My birth plan. . ." Amanda gestured toward the folder poking out of her backpack and tried to not feel foolish. Written guides of stretch positions, breathing patterns, how she wanted to skip

medication until the last moment, truly experience the beauty of childbirth. How she wanted to never have the baby leave her side, no matter what. How she planned to get over her nervousness about the breastfeeding and embrace natural parenting. All of it suddenly seemed a cruel, sick joke.

Doctor A glanced at the folder and clicked her tongue, dismissing it as if she knew every bit of the contents without reading it. Amanda didn't mention it again.

Three hours into labor, she gave up on the idea of calm breathing and stretching positions. She tried straddling the kidney-bean-shaped bouncing ball, but it did little to relieve her growing misery. At hour six, she allowed them to use some hideous contraption with an internal balloon and a dangling, weighted bag to help dilate her cervix. After her twelfth hour of labor, she caved in on the epidural and then the warm narcotic flow trickled through her veins and suddenly it wasn't so important that her birth plan had failed, that a baby the size of a small watermelon would have to push its way out of an impossibly small orifice. The hands on the clock started lying, started smearing, would jump in fits and starts.

Then it was happening, really happening, an awful pressure as if her bones were bending, on the verge of snapping, and she couldn't take it anymore, knew it was time even before Dr. A came bustling back into the room, looking like she'd run a marathon. The woman crouched in front of her between the stirrups, leaned in toward her open vulnerability with a bizarre hunger in the way her long fingers stretched out between Amanda's thighs, in her breathless accent as she murmured to push, to push, to push. In the mirror one of the nurses had positioned, Amanda watched a tuft of hair sprouting out of her swollen, straining body. Then a slimy, purplish head, and one more clenching squeeze that went on and on. . .and then the *whick* of a scalpel, a sudden stinging that pierced through the epidural, and the burden she'd carried for months flooded out of her in a sickening, emptying rush. It left behind a parting gift of a strangely hollow pain, as if she'd carved some part of herself off in order to create.

But all of the pain and blood and struggle was worth it.

The nurse set the baby on her naked chest, barely patted down with a towel and still sticky from the process, skin as thin as waterlogged tissue, the tiny twitch of fingers thinner than the eraser on the back of a pencil, tiny marshmallow toes little more than curling nubs. His face was a bit squished, the tuft of blonde hair matted down on his tiny skull and so far off center that it touched his comically miniature ear, but he was pudgy and pink and perfect. He smelled like heaven. His whimpers were a song.

Her baby.

And then Dr. A scooped the baby out from her arms and set it in the incubator cart, scribbling on a clipboard as she went. Amanda opened her mouth to protest but then the nurse was pushing on her stomach, forcing out the afterbirth, and she was trying her best to not vomit.

"Get some rest, Mom," the nurse said when she was finished. The doctor wheeled the cart toward the door. *"We'll take it from here."*

Amanda had tried not to panic, tried not to let the sudden terror rising inside her find shape or word as her precious prize vanished from sight. She wasn't one of *those girls*. She wasn't going to let birth drive her crazy. She'd seen her baby, and he was perfect and nothing else could go wrong.

Right?

Amanda shuddered and the memory fell apart into a hazy dream half-recalled. "He didn't have that."

She didn't need to specify what she meant.

The redhead nurse gave an apologetic toss of her ponytail. "Sure did. It's on his chart. It's called a prenatal tooth. It happens. Sometimes they even have a full set of chompers. Don't worry, it'll fall out in the first few days. Just your little fellow adjusting to the world."

But it wasn't just that either. His lopsided tuft of hair was gone. Amanda leaned in to sniff his head, but what had smelled heavenly barely an hour before now smelled slightly dusty. Dry. Almost sour. All those nature shows she'd watched over the past months showed mother animals nuzzling their young in something close to rapture. Not once did they show revulsion.

"Where did his hair go?"

The nurse shrugged. "Sometimes when they get their first bath, the hair falls out. If you think the birthing was hard for you, think about it from the baby's perspective. Pretty wild." The nurse leaned in to sniff too, and wrinkled her nose. "They might've missed a spot."

NESTING

Amanda watched her, searched for some indication that the woman was bluffing. All such simple explanations. Every bit of it made sense, had nurses and charts and doctors backing it up. She must've made a mistake about the tooth. They'd taken her baby so quickly, and she hadn't seen it. It didn't mean the baby wasn't hers, it didn't mean he was imperfect in any way. He was still her dream.

It just meant her dream had teeth.

"No," she whispered. "No."

Her hands were shaking, voice quavering and weak and she could barely make it out above the stampede of her heartbeat. *Not my baby.* The baby stared up at her and all at once the blank, nearly blind look seemed calculated and intelligent. A choked, guttural sound jerked its way out of her, and she shoved the gurney away with one weak hand.

The cart barely moved but the infant inside screwed up his face and began to whine in earnest, tooth jutting toward her at a grotesque, outward angle.

"Ma'am," the younger nurse began. She set her hand on the gurney and gently steered the disgruntled infant out of Amanda's reach. "You need to calm down."

Amanda fought back a snarl. *Calm* and *down* were two of the stupidest fucking words ever put together. "I'm not calm and I'm not going to be. You aren't listening. You got the wrong baby from the nursery. The wrong chart. Something. My name is Amanda—"

"Karen Amanda Carmichael. It's here in the charts along with everything else." The older of the two nurses gave her a flat, unfriendly look and Amanda realized that they definitely knew about her stay at St. Martin's. "That *is* your baby. There's no mistake. No confusion. The baby is yours. Doctor A is busy right now, but if you need me to get her. . ."

The woman said it like a threat.

Amanda shook her head. She opened her mouth, but struggled to find words. "Please," she managed at last, although she wasn't quite sure what she was pleading. Definitely not for the doctor.

Bates stared her down until Amanda found herself studying her hospital bracelet instead of meeting the woman's gaze. "You should be grateful for what you've got," the nurse continued. "Lots of woman wait their whole lives for the chance to be a mother."

Words custom-tailored to cut her to the bone—because Amanda knew she was right.

CHAPTER 3

AMANDA ALWAYS WANTED a baby.

Her little sister had a baby at seventeen, knocked up next to an occupied bathroom stall at her junior prom as best anyone could figure. Everyone else agreed that it was a tragedy, an embarrassment, a sick, cruel twist of bad fortune and bad decision.

Even back then, Amanda was jealous.

Jolie got a baby she could barely care for, and all it cost her was an uncomfortable couple of minutes bent over the sink, her hair dipping down into the dirty porcelain basin as she watched herself and her boyfriend of the week in the mirror, grunting and huffing away.

Amanda, seven years her senior and diligently toiling away as a school librarian, couldn't quite manage the trick. She had a steady boyfriend, a healthy, yoga-infused lifestyle, and she followed all the tips from charting her ovulation and her caloric intake to laying on her back after Ian finished inside her, her toes thrust up toward the ceiling as she took deep, slow breaths and he retreated to the bathroom to wipe himself off.

A baby.

That was all she had wanted, ever since she was seven years old and sat clutching a glassy-eyed plastic baby doll against herself while she watched her mother nurse her little sister, the two of them drowsing together on a cigarette-scarred yellow sofa in front of the television. She knew it in her bones, without question, without faltering. That was her purpose—to be a mom. When her mother carted them off to the overcrowded community church on Sunday, Amanda didn't spend her time pondering any great divine benevolence. Instead, she counted down the minutes to escape the incense-choked aroma of body odor and stared with envy at a stained-glass image of a mother in blue and white, cradling her child.

NESTING

Her teenage years were little more than a countdown.

She tried to fit in, but the other students worried about their parties, their sports, their careers, none of which interested Amanda. She was nothing special to look at, no great athlete, and her grades were, at best, described as unremarkable. Her mother made sure she remembered it, too. On the rare occasion she got invited out, she got the feeling she was mostly tolerated because she wasn't a threat and people pitied her.

She tried to take it as a compliment.

It wasn't, and she couldn't. She spent her first house party tormenting wide-eyed, drunken freshmen, murmuring awful, bloody stories that her father had brought home from deployment. Other kids got overpriced stuffed animals picked up in an airport when their parents came back from business trips. Amanda got stories of hook-handed killers, shape-shifting creatures lurking through the forest, monstrous changelings, a red-grinning Bloody Mary staring back through the mirror as she waited to hear her name three times. The only things she got of value from her father, she supposed. The only things he could share.

She spread the wealth.

The stories might have seemed silly during daylight, but hunched in pot-clouded basements in front of bleary-eyed teenagers on the cusp of puberty, she could feel them charge through her, fill her with the same anxiety they had when her father first rehearsed them. She infected her audience. She became something of a celebrity for it, among her classmates. Scarin' Karen, they called her. A fun act, enjoyed for a moment and then tossed aside as the night rolled out.

When she graduated, she left it all behind her along with her first name, but she realized she had never quite figured out how to make friends. Four lonely years of student loans later, she picked up a job as a grade-school librarian back home in Beaumont, at some faltering public school named Meadow Wood. Half the graduating classes never got the hang of reading, and the pay was a humiliating joke, but she got to work with children, could prepare her own nest, and year by year, she did. One day soon, she knew, she'd have a family of her own. Who needed friends then?

But the nest stayed empty.

Her first-year students grew, graduated, waved with fond—if slightly distant—recognition as they piled out of the sun-flooded gymnasium for the last time, eight years after first smiling up at her. She was an afterthought in their life now, as vague an entity as a babysitter they barely recognized. High school all over again.

Ian helped, but a steady boyfriend wasn't the same as actual family. Her father had proven that countless times to her mother.

She wept at her period, which only made the disappointment that much more barbed. If she could pretend it didn't hurt so much, it *wouldn't* hurt so much. If no one else could see the pain, it was almost like it wasn't really there. Almost.

The tears came just the same.

She scheduled appointments with specialists who shrugged and told her to keep trying, or offered up insultingly banal advice—was she aware that the time of the month heavily impacted likelihood of pregnancy? Did she know that diet played an important part? Had her family had a history of faulty genetics?—as if she hadn't studied every online article, as if she didn't keep a forest of ovulation tests beside her Q-tips and cotton balls above the toilet. She tried IUI, IVF, a swallow of some impotent holistic potion she found online that hadn't pretended to pass any FDA inspection. She had blood work drawn and egg samples taken and she sent Ian in for tests too, tests he passed with upsetting ease.

The bills rolled in without fail, but no baby. The specialists had no answers. Motherhood came hard to some, they said. There was little rhyme or reason. Just a game of odds. Had she considered adoption?

The thought was venomous.

Forget a hook for a hand, she'd have given her right arm for a baby all of her own. More, even.

Then, the incident.

Ian left. She didn't ask why. They both knew.

Thirty came and went, too. No husband, now no boyfriend, and still childless. Jolie popped out a third baby. A girl this time.

For a horrible six-month stretch Amanda tried to convince herself she was a pedophile. Six whole months. She spent her nights, dizzy and sick and half drunk on shitty boxed wine, her hand working between her thighs, trying to muster enthusiasm as she clicked around on clothing websites, looking at pictures of scrawny children in their underwear, scrolled through water park advertisements featuring boys and girls with their too-toothy grins and bright freckled faces, bathing suits clinging like Saran wrap to their shapeless frames.

If she could muster any hideous sense of lust, she supposed she'd be off the hook. Being that way and having children would be a monstrous crime, so the inability would be a blessing, right?

When the guilt became too much, she told herself instead that the world was no place for children anyway. That there'd come a time when she would be thankful for that monthly sucker punch of blood in her panties, that python squeeze of cramping as her latest crop of dreams died. She'd be okay. She could get used to it. That was life, wasn't it?

Ha-ha.

Jolie had her fourth child. Amanda discovered she liked the taste of tuna fish, mostly because her sister was allergic to it.

By the time she met Bobby—he had repaired her ancient, faltering air conditioning unit and the two of them hit it off right away—she was on the brink of surrender. He was a perfect candidate. He had no family history of mental illness or cancer, a steady job, and he didn't shy away from the idea of children without marriage. He treated her well too, had a sort of golden retriever energy that helped her relax. Her last shot. He moved in a month later.

Only now, watching him bustle in past the two nurses who stood sentry, still dressed in blue jeans and flannel and with a half dozen carnations in hand, she wondered if she should have just stuck with Bloody Mary and left the rest behind instead. Scary stories were so much easier to handle than scary truths.

"Hey babe!" Bobby said, taking absolutely no notice of the tension in the room and leaning over the baby. "You did it! Look at him! God, that's too cool."

He wiped his hands on his pants and scooped the baby up against his chest. His hand properly supported the head, Amanda noted absently. All those classes she made him take, paying off.

"Look at that. Too damn cool." He grinned at her, and she managed a weak smile in return. She wondered if the nurses had coached him somehow, if he knew she doubted the baby was hers. Maybe they planted him. Maybe he was in on it too. Maybe he had been all along. Maybe he was just one more skin-walking monster. Sick, diseased thoughts that made little to zero sense and, just the same, refused to quiet. Scarin' Karen murmuring away in her mind.

The baby began to cry. A high, choking sound.

"Oh! I bet he's hungry, Mom."

He turned to her and held the baby out, swaddled up in a blanket like some sort of twitching, mummified grub. Her lower lip trembled. She shook her head.

She couldn't feed him. If she nursed the baby, that would be the end of it. How could she claim it wasn't hers, if she nursed it? Maybe they all knew that too. Maybe they were all conspiring together. . .

She was too tired to muster any real emotion at the idea. Her battery was used up.

Bobby nudged her with his hip. "What's wrong, babe?"

"Nothing," Amanda managed. "I'm fine."

"The baby needs to feed," said old Ms. Bates. "Doctor A won't be happy if you can't feed him. I can send Lisa here to go get her."

Again, spoken like a threat.

The redheaded nurse flinched. "Lactation," she said. "How about I go get a lactation consultant instead?"

Without waiting for approval, she fled.

CHAPTER 4

THE LACTATION CONSULTANT was a heavyset, motherly woman in straining scrubs with a large black satchel in one hand. She bustled in with an air of purpose.

"Out," she said, and out Bobby went. He blew Amanda a kiss as he left. The older nurse shot Amanda a final, irritated glance before following him out. The door closed behind her.

"Thanks," Amanda said when they were gone.

"We're gonna get you all sorted out, okay? You ready?"

Amanda allowed a tiny nod. It was inevitable. She was going to need to nurse the baby, had come to accept that while waiting for the consultant to arrive, but not with Bobby and the nurses watching her betrayal. The boy moaned and wriggled in his bassinet beside her.

"Alright Ms.. . ." she checked the chart. "Karen? May I call you that? They said you're having trouble with nursing?"

Amanda flinched. "Amanda," she said. "I'm not Karen anymore." She tried to say more, but wasn't sure what was left to say.

The woman smiled. "Amanda, then. It really is best for the child," she said. "It helps their immune systems in a way that formula can't, it leads to bonding and they're far less likely to have any issue with. . .the unexpected."

SIDS. Death. Cancerous, monstrous words that only the cruelest would dare say to a new mother, words that hung like a bloated black thundercloud at the corners of her vision. Amanda nodded along. She knew all that. It wasn't like she had skimped on those anxieties over the past decades.

"It's not that, it's just. . ."

The nurse gave her hand a gentle squeeze.

"It's going to be okay. A lot of mothers are nervous about it. An easy trick is to tent a light blanket over the baby. Loose enough that it can move and breathe, but so you can't see. It's easier if you don't fixate on it."

"Okay," Amanda said.

The woman nodded in satisfaction. "Let's see what you've got going on here," she said.

Amanda reluctantly peeled down her gown. She'd never had much in the way of breasts, had lived her life as a grudging A cup until she was pregnant, when they had swollen up, painful and awkward.

"None of that, Mom. Nursing your child is nothing to be ashamed about. Anyone tells you differently, I'll have words with them."

Amanda blinked back unexpected tears.

Bobby had been entranced by her transformation, but she'd always found it a bit appalling. They looked wrong. They hurt. The thought of him touching them made her feel physically ill.

"Thanks," she said again. The consultant ignored her.

"Here," she placed the baby against Amanda's skin. She gripped Amanda's hands and moved her into position. Amanda tried not to notice the sour, musty smell that lingered around the baby like a rotting halo. "Like so. We'll try football carry if this doesn't work, but this usually works."

And suddenly she felt it, the baby rooting around, its tiny mouth suctioning against her skin, wet and soft and probing. The tooth was there—she could feel its strange hardness tickling against her sensitive skin—but it wasn't all that bad, she told herself. Weird and gross and it definitely wasn't comfortable, but the baby wasn't biting. When little Bobby found his goal and she felt the stinging tug of her let-down, she clenched her jaw until the feeling passed.

But she found herself cradling the baby against her body, in spite of it all. As if the tiny pink bundle could provide a warmth that no number of blankets could generate. In some way it helped ease her doubts. Maybe, she decided, that's what had worried her the most.

The consultant gave her a gentle pat on the shoulder.

"You're doing the right thing, you know. You want your baby to grow up healthy and strong."

Amanda peeked down at the infant suckling greedily away.

"What if. . ." she glanced at the door. No sound leaked through from the outside, so they shouldn't be able to hear her. She lowered her voice just the same. "What if it isn't mine?"

The consultant fiddled in her bag, sorting through pockets packed full of pads, creams, strange plastic cups and jars. She did not look up as she spoke. "The baby is yours, Amanda. You have some of the best nurses and doctors in the state looking after you. Everyone here is on your team, okay? You went through a lot the last couple days. The last couple months, really. A gunshot wound has nothing on delivering a baby. Believe me, I've worked in ERs, and I've worked here, and this thing puts you through the ringer. It's beautiful, but it's a lot."

The bed creaked as she leaned her weight against it, gave Amanda's shoulder a gentle squeeze.

"I'm not crazy," Amanda said. It came out a whisper. Scarin' Karen's voice.

"I would never say that. We don't even use that word here." She paused and Amanda was certain she was deciding whether to leave the baby in her arms or scoop it up and sweep it away. Strangely, the thought filled her with an even deeper panic. Being alone was worse than being with something wrong. Instead, she gave Amanda's shoulder another kindly pat. "What would help ease your mind?"

"I. . .don't know." It was difficult to swallow. "Maybe check with the other mothers? You see all the babies, right? Mine was a baby with blonde hair, no tooth, that um. . .that. . ." she trailed off. She couldn't think of any other description. *That smells good?*

The consultant indulged her with a gentle smile. "Certainly, dear. If that will help. But it is yours. Every part of the chart matches up, and Dr A is extremely thorough. She likes to work every step of the process. She even draws the blood and fills out the paperwork, from birth until the baby is out the door. You don't ever find doctors these days who do that. These specialists nowadays make nurses do it all, but not Doctor A. It'll be a shame to see her go."

"Go where?"

"She's a hospital hopper. Travels. In a couple weeks she'll be on to the next one. She says they pay better that way and I don't think she has family."

Amanda stayed quiet. She wasn't sure what to ask, what she needed to hear to banish the buzzing nervousness in her mind. *Did she steal my baby? Does she have a face underneath the mask?*

"What's she like?"

"She's very good at what she does. Not very friendly though. You know how those types are."

Amanda nodded, not at all sure what the woman meant, but afraid to ask. The consultant was the first one who didn't look at her like she was the villain. Or some lunatic. The first one who didn't make her want to cram her fingers through their eyes and claw a hole so she could shout directly into their brains that she wasn't crazy, she wasn't wrong. That the baby wasn't hers, wasn't hers, *wasn't hers*, they swapped it and they lied and she was just so tired.

The consultant hesitated before continuing, a flush staining her cheeks. "A bunch of the nurses are a little bit scared of her. Not me, of course, but. . .a bunch of them. If you really want to hear it from the source, I guess I could always ask her to stop by."

Her tone seemed to suggest that it was a nearly unthinkable idea.

The baby wriggled against Amanda, clammy heat against her bare skin, and she did her best not to push the infant away. If it truly was as simple as they all said and she was just getting squeamish at the finish line, she had to know. She took a deep breath in and let it out. Her hands were shaking.

"Okay then," she said at last. "Go get the doctor."

CHAPTER 5

WHEN THE CONSULTANT left, Amanda was alone again. With the baby, but still alone.

She'd spent most of her life alone. She hated it.

The tired little apartment of her childhood had seemed both too small and too big at the same time, too cramped for her to relax but also friendless and lonely and empty. Her mother spent most of the day in front of the television, eyes half closed and a blanket thrown across her knees as she watched shows about hospitals where everyone seemed to want to kiss each other. Her father was deployed overseas as often as not. Nothing in her life seemed to fit. Hours whiled away with toys she'd outgrown, TV that she'd not yet grown into, and a listless anxiety that clung to her like ivy.

Her sister's arrival changed all that. Her mother transformed from a bored automaton shuffling through existence into something vibrant. The house went from neglected to polished, clean and proper and orderly. Bland soap operas were replaced with brightly colored cartoons, lessons about Jesus, and animal documentaries featuring men with thick Australian accents. Her father still favored armed combat over coming home, but suddenly there was a sense of family around the house that had never been there previously. As if now—and only now—they were a family.

It had seemed so strange to Amanda how her mother's entire outlook on life could hinge on something so simple as a baby, and she had always wondered what it was that Jolie provided, but Amanda failed to supply.

After her stint in St. Martin's, she understood.

She was twenty-nine when she had the miscarriage. Not *her* miscarriage, *the*. The distinction was important. And it wasn't much of a miscarriage. Not even seven weeks, well before she dared tell anyone. She kept the baby her secret, so she kept the absence a secret too. It wasn't like she'd lost it after three months. That happened to people. She'd seen the pictures, had read the heartbroken blog posts. It was an ugly and terrible thing, but she didn't have to think about a coffin sized for a sparrow, didn't have to see tiny bent limbs as she birthed a nightmare. Other women had it worse.

Maybe.

Sitting on the toilet with a shapeless clot of strange, bloody mess the size of a plum's pit bobbing up and down in the cloudy surf beneath her, she wasn't sure. It might as well have been her soul there.

The shame was the worst part, and so she faced it alone.

She never told her mom, never told her sister. Never went to a hospital, never told a single soul. She kept the vision of that poor unfortunate thing in the gore-stained water to herself, buried it down within her heart and out of the light.

A few weeks later, it began to grow.

She had her first panic attack while driving to work, her heart squeezing, hands shaking, sounds drowned out as if the radio was broadcasting to her through a womb-bubble of fluid, the car horns a distant thrumming, and then she was stopped in the middle of the interstate and a police officer was knocking on her window and she collapsed onto the exhaust-poisoned asphalt and vomited. She called in sick, tried to get some rest, but found no peace there either. In her dreams, the feeling sprouted from her mouth, mucus-slickened bark spreading her jaw until she choked and sputtered and the joints snapped out of their sockets, the branches unfolding and black leaves blossoming as she strangled. When she did make it into work and dozed behind her desk, she felt the baby kicking inside her. Clawing. Chewing. She lasted a week before she committed herself.

Other people went to rehab for their partying habits. Amanda went to St. Martin's because if she didn't, she knew she was going to end up floating in the blood-filled bathtub, her forearms opened from wrist to elbow in a sloppy, split mouth, just one more poor unfortunate thing swimming in a porcelain pool of red. The real Bloody Mary.

Officially, she took a vacation.

She didn't tell anyone, didn't say a word when Ian walked out the door for the last time, shaking his head in confusion at her sudden inability to touch him, to confess where she'd been for the past three weeks. There was nothing for him to say anyway, and only danger in her speaking the words and giving them flesh.

Who would dare risk trying to have children with her if they found out?

No one could know.

No one except every nurse in the hospital. Every doctor. It was written in their charts. Her greatest failure, immortalized. Every one of them had seen through her disguise. Every one of them knew she was *that girl*.

The door whispered open and closed, Bobby collapsing onto the sofa next to her, his eyes glued to his phone. If he noticed she was awake, he didn't give any indication. She dreaded the thought of a voice breaking the silence, of lungs pulling in air to ruin what little rest she could salvage, so she said nothing.

She dozed, flitting from one unhappy memory to the next, examining them like tarot cards—Ian leaving was a nine of swords, the psych ward was the tower—and was finally, tantalizingly near sleep when she sensed someone else in the room with her. She wasn't sure when the stranger had entered, only that she wasn't there one bleary blink and the next she was. Amanda's heart gave an unhappy jerk, sent the vibrating swarm of anxiety to buzzing again through her chest. Her mind felt bruised, wounded, a limping animal in its last struggles, denied even the peace of a moment's rest.

Doctor A stood over her, arms folded, dark eyes peering down from above her darker mask.

"Ms. Carmichael."

"Huh?" Amanda wiped at the corners of her mouth, marveled at the name on her hospital bracelet as a touchstone. Seeing her name in print helped. "My students call me that. My name's Amanda."

Bobby coughed and sat up and Amanda realized he must've been sleeping too.

"Jeez," he said. "You snuck up on me. My name is—" Bobby cleared his throat, stood, offered his hand, and was promptly ignored.

Dr A clicked her tongue. "Ms. Carmichael, the nurses tell me you've been causing problems."

The doctor wasn't quite tall enough to loom, but Amanda still found herself instinctively shrinking back, pushing with her heels to drive herself deeper into the mattress. The woman reminded her vaguely of some sort of predatory, long-beaked bird, with eyes like shiny buttons. Nothing maternal here. No softness like the lactation consultant. No compassion. Like she was made of rope instead of meat. Amanda tried to imagine the doctor squatting down in a nest, but instead of a silly way to push away the nervousness it made her think of that dream from so long ago, where the awful tree burst out of her mouth. Amanda swallowed before finding her voice.

"No, no, I'm not," Amanda said. Everything she said or did felt sluggish, outpaced and weak. It wasn't a fair matchup. She wasn't at her best. She shook her head—slowly—and tried to meet the small woman's gaze. "I promise. I'm just. . ."

She couldn't find the words. She wondered if anyone ever died from sheer exhaustion, but that was dangerously close to the line of thought that landed her in the ward all those years ago, so she shied away from wondering too hard.

"She's just tired, doctor." Bobby said. He reached out and patted Amanda's hand, his fingers warm and dry. Amanda flinched. "Neither of us want to be a problem. No problem at all," he said.

Dr. A clicked her tongue again. She did not so much as glance at him.

"This baby is yours."

"But isn't it possible—"

Dr. A held a hand up in firm refusal. "No. I took your baby to the nursery myself. I personally drew the blood for labs. We know how many children we have on the unit. No babies can leave without us noticing. No way for them to disappear."

"It could have been swapped with another mother's."

"No other mother complains. Only yours has a tooth. Don't you remember?"

Amanda shook her head.

But. . .did she? She tried to go back to the memory of holding her newborn child, breathing in the smell of him, the first attempt at nursing him, but did she ever look inside his mouth? Were mothers supposed to do that? Her thoughts were a fumbled juggling act, all hazy and strange whenever they edged toward the night before. She could remember a dream from a decade ago, but she couldn't quite recall her baby's mouth. She was too tired, too used up. The stitching in her body and mind all felt loose. If she were better held together...

"Can I at least check the nursery?"

"She's joking," Bobby said. He raised his hands in a placating gesture, shot her an alarmed sidelong glance—*What the fuck, Amanda?*—that the doctor could clearly see.

Dr A clicked her tongue again, arms folded across her flat chest. "No. You will stay here, in this room. You will take care of your baby. If you can't, I'll send in a nurse to sit with you. But this business will stop. Now. The baby is yours. You need to feed him so that he can grow and be healthy. And he *must* grow and be healthy. Do you understand?"

She felt herself nodding along. "Yes, doctor." Her voice sounded small. She wasn't sure which part she was agreeing to.

Bobby was watching her too. Waiting for something. She wanted to scream, to squeeze her eyes shut, to get up and fight, to do. . .something. She didn't know what. To throw back some otherworldly curtain and find that feeling of wonder when she first held her baby in her arms and point at them all and judge them and have them accept that she was right. She *wasn't* crazy. She knew it in her heart.

Her lower lip trembled, and it was all she could do to keep from bursting into tears.

"It's my baby," she mumbled. "It's my baby. It's my baby."

Bloody Mary. Bloody Mary. Bloody Mary.

Doctor A nodded. Behind her mask, she might have smiled, but Amanda couldn't tell.

CHAPTER 6

AMANDA WAITED UNTIL an hour before shift change.

An hour before was just the right amount of time. Earlier, and the night nurse might still plan on stopping by to check on her, make one last pass before her shift ended and she gave report. Much after an hour, and she risked running out of time. An hour before though, that was the perfect window to sneak around.

She'd learned a thing or two at St. Martin's.

Besides, the baby seemed to feed just about every hour, and she didn't mean to be out of the room when he woke up and started howling.

Once little Bobby had fallen asleep, milk-drunk and belching and briefly satisfied, she settled in and waited, forced her breathing to stay steady and her eyes half-closed. She was worried, at first, that she might accidentally fall asleep. She didn't need to worry much. The stammering in her chest wouldn't yield any relief, and as weary and wounded as she was, her mind was like a spinning wheel and nothing could slow it enough for proper rest. She watched the rise and fall of Bobby's chest as he snored, slumped across the cushioned bench, with a jagged, caustic sort of envy that bordered up against hate.

He was sleeping fine. Of course he was. He'd had a long day at work fixing air conditioning units. He might've even had paperwork to fill out.

She gritted her teeth. It wasn't his fault, she told herself. Her misery didn't require other people to be miserable. Some bullshit reversal of the motivational speeches she used to listen to once a month when she woke up to a sanitary pad soaked in foul-smelling blood. *Your happiness isn't dependent on anyone else's happiness. You are in charge of your own destiny and your own satisfaction.*

Well, she was going to be in charge tonight.

The door swung open on silent, well-greased hinges. A head peeked in, the black shape a shadow cut out against the darker room. Amanda could feel the nurse visually assessing her, confirming that she was asleep and the baby safe and snug in the crib and then the door settled shut.

She counted to a hundred, then forced her legs over the side of the bed.

Standing hurt. She didn't let herself think about the stinging, throbbing ache between her thighs, the pain in her stomach, the loudness of her shuffling feet as they whispered across the floor. Those weren't things she could control. She was in charge of her own destiny, not how other people reacted. If either of the other two woke up. . .she decided to not think about it.

She paused at the door to brace herself, to beg any powers that were watching over her to let the hallway be empty, and then she slipped out and eased the door shut behind her.

All those years getting dragged in to church may have paid out after all. The hall was empty. The fluorescent overheads were dimmed to simulate night for the patients, but without windows it felt more like an abandoned hotel, curiously sinister in its attempt at artificial comfort. Door after door lined either side, thick oaken things that could muffle the sound of babies crying, or of patients sobbing in pain. The checkered flooring stretched before her as she shuffled along.

Everything looked unfamiliar. She hadn't left her room since her arrival, but it all felt different from her hazy recollection of the day before. An imitation as flawed as the baby beside her bed. She ground her teeth as she shoved strings of unwashed hair from her face. The placards on the wall helped her find where she needed to go, and she made her way through the maze as quickly as she dared. She tried to remember her room number, couldn't, and briefly considered turning around to go check, but it was too late for that.

If she went back now, she would lose her nerve.

It was all too easy to imagine the maternity ward as the psych ward, that getting caught could lead to the men in white coats and cuffs and a needle full of midazolam. She tried to remind herself that it wasn't like that in a maternity ward, that it was never like that in St. Martin's either—only violently dangerous people got the restraints or injections, and she wasn't one of those, was she? Was she?—but all she could think about was the Spiderlady and that was enough to override any logic.

Amanda had heard stories at St. Martin's about the Spiderlady. Everyone had, it seemed. The rumor was that years back, when the ward was far less voluntary and far less supervised, one of the girls had taken to plucking her teeth out, one by one, and filing them down into lockpicks so she could trip her restraints and roam the halls.

She would break out of her room just about every night and go crawling down the corridors on all fours, naked and cackling and biting, bloody-mouthed, at the orderlies who tried to restrain her. She would hide all over—nesting in a mop-cluttered maintenance closet one night, grinning up with wide, wet eyes from beneath a howling patient's bed the next. They moved her from room to room, trying to find a way to keep her locked in, but come nighttime she'd be out again, giggling and barking, bare white ass all wrinkled and scabby as she scuttled about and snarled and howled. Finally, someone pumped her full of enough sedatives that she never woke back up, or so the story went.

Only, some part of her teeth must have broken off in the locks, because the doors never locked quite right in the rooms they'd kept her, and if you listened at night, you could sometimes still hear a high-pitched chitter of angry delight. And if you snuck out after curfew—and sneaking out after curfew was one of the few excitements on the ward—you might just find yourself in a hallway with a pale figure squatting at the far end. She might just go bounding toward you, drooling and gibbering and screaming, not toothless anymore, but her mouth a mess of crusted hypodermic needles.

If she caught your scent, you couldn't ever really get away anyway. She had a trick for unlocking the doors. She could always find her way in. . .

Amanda heard the legend so often that she found herself telling others that she had seen the Spiderlady too and wasn't quite sure she was lying. If Bloody Mary could hold her own against logic, and the hook-handed killer persisted, why not the Spiderlady? They swapped stories like trading cards, even harassed the staff about it at their group sessions when they all sat around in those miserably uncomfortable folding metal chairs, elbows on knees and unwilling to make eye contact.

NESTING

There was no Spiderlady, of course. Amanda understood that. There never had been. She figured most of the other patients staying at St. Martin's knew it too. The hospital was barely three decades old, not some dark-historied sanitarium. The logistics of teeth as lockpicks was shaky at best, and there was no reason to think she'd want to hurt anyone even if she had existed. There was magic in the myth, though. The same Scarin' Karen magic that had powered her those long years before. When it came her chance to whisper the story to the new arrivals—and there was a constant, revolving door of new arrivals—they didn't just idly listen. They leaned in.

There had been a comfort in charging them up with the same old spell.

It helped the nurses with keeping new patients in bed at night too, and she half wondered if the rumor hadn't been started intentionally by one of the staff.

The old magic was no longer a comfort. Her head ached too much for her to parse out any excitement in the idea of the woman prowling along, naked, her yellowed nails clicking on the tiles. She was too tired, everything too blurry at the edges, and it didn't seem so impossible that the Spiderlady could be there too, in the hazy twilight of the hospital. That she might sniff Amanda out and her eyes wouldn't be rheumy and squinting from all those years of wandering. They'd be gaping caverns with a single tooth waggling in their depths. And instead of a dentureless maw, she'd be muzzled behind a rigid black mask.

Amanda shuddered.

Doctor A was just a person. Probably just nervous about infection. That didn't make her sinister. Hell, maybe she was pretty, Amanda told herself. She somehow doubted it.

She turned the corner and the front desk came into view, but the nurse on duty was drowsing, slouched back in his chair, his phone balanced on his chest. He didn't look up as she drifted by, quiet as a ghost.

The dimmed lights worked in her favor. Even if they'd been talking about her, with the lights low enough, she would be just another patient. One more mother trying out her badly wounded body to see if the ol' engine was still able to turn. There was nothing wrong about walking the halls. She hadn't done anything wrong. Yet. No Spiderlady after her.

Then she could see the steel-framed double doors ahead of her, sealed and locked for anyone without a badge, and her mouth was suddenly dry. She tried to casually lean against the wall, but she was aware that at some point the front desk nurse would look up and see her, that her intentions were painfully obvious. She should have brought her phone, a mask, something to hide herself so no one would think twice about her skulking near the nursery entrance, waiting for someone to leave and let her slip in.

A few feet ahead she noticed the door to a break room yawning open and she slipped inside without thinking.

She was halfway through the doorway before she noticed that the room was occupied.

Amanda barely registered any of it—the plastic fern that made only a feeble effort at imitating life, the coffee station with its waterlogged sugar packets, the bland framed pictures and bland empty countertops—barely noticed anything at all besides the figure seated at the table.

Doctor A sat with her back to the doorway, lips smacking as she hunched over her meal, a meaty block—ribs? steak?—the thickness of Amanda's fist.

There was something primal and unwholesome about it all, the wet, tearing meat, the occasional grunt of pleasure. Amanda was suddenly sure that the meat was rare and marbled with fatty knots of gristle, that bloody juices were running in pink, greasy rivulets between the webbing of her fingers and down her wrists as she gobbled it down. That her chin was slathered with the mess as she tore off each tattered bite.

If Amanda had wondered what the doctor's face looked like before, she sure didn't now. She didn't want to know, didn't want to see. It seemed very important that it stay a mystery.

Amanda's vision swam, a tunnel of strange shadows writhing at the edges, and she stepped backwards as silently as she could manage, her heartbeat echoing in a throbbing agony that lit up her groin with each thunderous pulse.

Her foot was out the door when the woman stiffened. Her slovenly chewing stopped.

Amanda stepped outside and pressed herself against the wall, palms slick with sweat and prayers forming on her lips, but she didn't allow herself to think them. In case the doctor would somehow know. In case Amanda would see the woman crane around the edge of the door on a too-long neck, her face a noseless tangle of deranged teeth that filled up every inch that her mask had hidden. Vertigo spilled over her in waves.

A chair inside creaked and Amanda was sure that the doctor was staring off toward her.

The dark-eyed woman couldn't see through the wall, she reminded herself. Amanda might as well be invisible. *Not crazy!* she insisted to herself, but it seemed like a losing battle.

A moment later, the wet chewing returned and she allowed herself to breathe, flopped against the wallpaper, weak with sweaty relief.

There were footsteps too, and she had only a moment to remind herself why she had snuck out in the first place before the double doors to the nursery swung open.

Two nurses strolled past, heads tilted toward each other and quietly murmuring as they passed a phone back and forth between them. She thought one might have been the redhead from earlier—Lisa, was it?—but neither paid her any notice as she slipped past them and stepped inside.

CHAPTER 7

THE NURSERY WAS nothing like she imagined it.

Amanda had always pictured those old movies with the parents peering through a glass window, ogling their babies, recognizing them and cooing to them with all the effect of a detective looking into an interrogation room, but in reality it was a wide-open floor with smiling posters on the walls, a collection of reminders and bulletin boards weighted down with notices, desks for the nurses and empty plastic seats that seemed like they'd better fit in a first-grade classroom.

She wondered why, during all those years researching pregnancy, she'd spent so little time looking up the details that mattered.

The babies lay in two parallel rows of plastic tubs far away from any of the walls, rigid mattresses beneath them, dim white light illuminating the room. Monitors slept beside them, IV trees with nothing in their branches cast hatch-mark shadows across the unscuffed floor. The whole room felt like a set from a movie of some hyper-idealized futuristic spacecraft. Cleanliness like godliness, babies all tagged and in orderly pods. Her mother would be so impressed.

Around the edges of the room, closed doors couldn't completely muffle the BEEP BEEP BEEP of monitors, alarms monitoring the breathing and heart rate of the less fortunate babies who needed more specialized care. An elderly nurse paced behind a series of monitors, clipboard in hand as she strolled back and forth, back and forth.

If she recognized Amanda, she gave no indication. In the low light, the ancient woman might as well have been a ghost dressed in scrubs, pacing restlessly up and down the tiny plastic cells. Maybe she was a ghost, Amanda supposed. Shouldn't a place like this be haunted? If St. Martin's had the Spiderlady, there should be ghosts all over here, specters of the babies who didn't make it, of the heartbroken mothers searching forever for their dead young, the corpses of nurses floating their way through one last shift, despite leaving their bodies slumped over in the medicine closet with veins or bellies full of drugs.

Amanda approached as far as she dared, just close enough to study each face, one by one, as she circled the island of cribs.

What was she even looking for? Six babies weren't nearly enough. Shouldn't there be more? The rest. . .the rest might be in those side rooms, the isolation rooms for babies too sick to interact. Or maybe her baby was in another recovery room, some strange woman mashing the face of Amanda's dream against her breast.

The image caused the nausea to spike up again. Hormones, she told herself. Hormones. She wasn't acting crazy, it was just. . .her thoughts skittered away from her. Something in her was just a little untethered ever since they'd lost her baby. That was all. She tried to focus on the task at hand.

And then she'd completed her circuit. Six newborn infants, their mouths seemingly without teeth, their tiny faces so relaxed in sleep that it was hard to tell that they were living, breathing things and not a line of dolls laid out to convince passing mothers that all was well.

She shook her head and reminded herself to focus on the task at hand. *Always place the mission first.* That's what her father had taught her first and foremost. Some parents taught their kids the ABCs and what sound a giraffe makes—she still was somewhat uncertain on that last one, despite copious amounts of *Animal Planet*—but not Amanda's dad. Her dad had been an Airborne Ranger, and he thought there were more important lessons. She wondered what mission he'd placed first when he never came home after the Army shipped him out to Japan. He wasn't dead or wounded, he simply liked it better there and decided to set up shop after he'd retired from serving.

She considered another circuit around the babies, but without much motivation.

Each child was perfect and pretty and none of them were hers. She pressed her lips shut to keep a low moan from spilling out of her.

Of course they weren't hers.

Hadn't she known that all along? Isn't that what the nurses said? The doctor, Bobby, all the charts and paperwork agreed, too. Her baby was back in her room, sleeping soundly. What was she doing?

She felt her certainty wavering, clenched her hands into sweat-slickened fists as if she could menace the doubts away. *That girl.* Just some crazy woman. Forget seeing ghosts, she was one step away from being the Spiderlady herself.

"I'm not," she whispered. "I'm not her."

The words felt heavy in her mouth, did nothing to dispel the suffocating weight of dread. Of defeat.

She wished she were back in her room, that she'd never dared check, but it didn't matter now. She couldn't stop. She had to know. And if she did find her baby, she would grab him and. . .and. . .

She refused to think about the men with their needles and restraint cuffs.

She headed to the side rooms next. She knew what she'd find. Unlike the pink, healthy sleepers in the center room, the babies inside were hooked up to strange tubes and monitors, plastic veins sprouting out of new orifices that had been neatly punched into throats, into stomachs, half-translucent cotton-soft skin puckered around IVs and taped-up ports, the slightest peek of dull red muscle beneath the clear plastic. Like rare steak. The thought came before she could stop herself.

None of them were her baby. There wasn't some conspiracy, there was just Karen, just *that girl*, just her mother looking back from the reflections in the stainless-steel equipment like the original Bloody Mary.

As she left the second of the isolated side rooms, the nursery double doors swung open. She spun away so they wouldn't spot her, tried to slip back inside with the tiny sacks of tube-fed meat, but the footsteps padded forward only one pace more before they stopped.

She knew whose footsteps before they spoke. She felt like the floor was crumbling beneath her feet.

"Ms. Carmichael," Doctor A said. She clicked her tongue in sharp disapproval and Amanda's pulse gave an unhappy jolt. "What are you doing in here?"

CHAPTER 8

SHORTLY AFTER SUNRISE they sent her home.

Baby Bobby passed the car seat test with ease—had he grown already? He seemed fuller, plumper, and louder—and spent the next few hours plastered to her breasts, slurping away. Bobby the boyfriend pestered her with slightly deranged questions from a checklist—did she intend to take up smoking? To drink? To use hard drugs? Did she plan to suffocate her baby with blankets, to roll on top of it and smother it to death while co-sleeping?

She wondered if anyone ever said "Yes."

At no point was she left alone. No one spoke the accusations, no one filed any complaints, but it just so happened that, without fail, someone in scrubs always hovered in the corner of her vision, watching her carefully and taking notes. No needles or cuffs, but Amanda got the message loud and clear that it was still an option. When she shambled off to the bathroom to take a shit and felt her stitches tugging at her distorted, sore body, an old, no-nonsense nurse accompanied her, helped her stand and wipe—there was so much red—and re-dress herself.

Amanda accepted the treatment without complaint.

She accepted the small stack of pamphlets that were pressed into her hands too, glossy, thin pages filled with titles like "postpartum anxiety," "depression," and "re-claiming yourself."

The lactation consultant paid one last visit, and then Amanda was shuffling out the door, a nurse on either side of her and streaks of fire lancing through her crotch with each step. Bobby held the baby, strapped into the car seat. Her bags were looped over his shoulders, bags that had once been so lovingly packed by a girl who felt oddly distant. Maybe, she thought, the baby belonged to that happier, naïve girl. Maybe he hadn't been swapped out.

Maybe she had.

She hoped she wasn't forgetting anything. She had a sense that it wouldn't be returned, and that once she was out the doors, the doors would lock and stay shut. Her welcome was used up. *She* was used up.

It was hard to feel anything at all as she stepped out into the chilly morning sunlight and made her way over to her Acura. The air inside was nauseatingly stale and vaguely flatulent from the bag of French fries Bobby had left, half-eaten, on the passenger seat floor while she was in labor.

Bobby helped her into the backseat as gently as he could, then set about clicking the car seat into the base. It hurt to sit. It hurt to buckle herself in. Every part of her body seemed to throb and ache, flickers of discomfort lighting up through her like Christmas lights, and she knew it was going to be a misery of a car ride, that each bump, each pebble passing beneath the tires, every gentle swerve within the lanes would set a phantom of pressure haunting her wounded body.

The engine coughed to life, vents blasted out their lifeless heat, the blinker chimed and then there was no more time and they were pulling out and leaving, the hospital fading behind them. Amanda couldn't be sure if the weight in her stomach was relief or acceptance, and she found it remarkable how similar they felt. In the car seat next to her, the baby stirred in his sleep.

If she looked back, she was suddenly sure she would see Doctor A peering down from her hospital window roost, the light behind her bright enough to keep her features a shadowy mess in the dull dawn, a faceless specter following her with dark, empty eyes.

She shivered, brought her gaze down to the baby instead. Her baby.

They'd made her rehearse it again and again before they let her leave. It was that or getting assigned a caseworker.

For the first time, though, it sounded almost right.

My baby. My baby. My baby.

With each repetition, the disbelief that had hovered around her like a swarm of flies lighted up and buzzed through her brain before settling back down, their presence growing slightly weaker as the minutes gave way to miles.

All the while Bobby asked her questions about the birthing and listed all the stuff they still needed to buy and other unimportant things. She decided that it was worth it. Her baby was worth it. The chaotic fever dream of the last few days could stay behind, because that's all it really was. A bizarre nightmare. Happiness waited for her. The life she always wanted.

They were halfway home and she was nearly smiling when the wrinkly pink potato next to her blinked up at her in bleary irritation, screwed up his face and began to howl.

The eggshell bony nub of his tooth wiggled as he shook with rage.

CHAPTER 9

"**W**ELCOME HOME," Bobby announced as he flung the door open.

His attempts at enthusiasm had noticeably dampened over the last ten minutes of the car ride. Amanda couldn't blame him.

Baby Bobby's bellowing had reached a migraine-inducing pitch, a miniature irate prisoner in ear-splitting protest of his position. By the time she unclipped him from his seat, his tiny hands were wrapped into purple fists and his face glistened with tears. The whites of his eyes were streaked with red.

"You already ate at the hospital. That wasn't even half an hour ago," Amanda gently chided him, but she couldn't help feeling a strange pang of something that bordered on enjoyment. He didn't just want anyone. He didn't want some other mother. He wanted *her*. And didn't that prove it more than anything else? He was *hers*. Being wanted was being loved. Right?

She'd be glad when she was finished with the nursing, but she doubted she would ever tire of being needed that purely.

Home was a single-floor rancher, the décor as chic as her teacher's salary could afford. The carpets bought on discount from Target, spiderwebbed cracks in the walls that she never got around to spackling, lamps that did not match taking the place of an overhead light. A floral sofa in the den—picked up from one of the local furniture stores that perpetually claimed to be liquidating all stock—with a Christmas quilt draped across the back. Amanda limped her way inside and dropped immediately onto the couch. She winced at the pain in her pelvis and wondered, briefly, if it was ever going to stop. She placed the baby beside her, too worn out to walk him over to the bassinet. It was no easy task, moving.

NESTING

Baby Bobby continued to scream, wrinkly little hands groping toward her, fingers thrust out like tiny pink hooks.

While boyfriend Bobby checked the fridge, Amanda unbuttoned her shirt and pulled the baby boy onto her lap, tented the quilt up and over him and guided him up against her tender flesh. She stared at the quilt, studied the yarn depiction of partridges perched in pear trees amid a backdrop of laughing Santa heads. A silly, stupid thing that Jolie had given her as a present the year past, but staring at the decapitated Kris Kringles beat thinking about what was going on beneath.

"Your sister dropped off a ton of food," Bobby said. "She offered to come by and help out for a bit, if you'd like."

Amanda sniffed herself and wrinkled her nose. She could imagine what she looked like.

"No," she said. "I can do this."

"Okay, babe," he called back.

Amanda had spent so much time reading about the difficulties of breast feeding that she was still startled to realize baby Bobby knew exactly what he was doing. Barely two days old and it took him only a moment of rooting around to find her nipple and latch on. He set to eating with a concentration that would have been admirable if not for the revulsion skittering across the floor of her stomach.

Draining her.

She pushed the thought away.

It was gross, sure, but so what? The blanket helped. The bony protrusion dragging across her skin felt vaguely obscene, but it wasn't a big deal. She thought she could get used to it.

She was going to be happy, she decided. She needed to be happy. Needed to not be crazy.

She would throw those silly pamphlets out as soon as she could stand up and move. She didn't have postpartum anything. She'd learn to enjoy breast feeding. She wouldn't worry about the squeezing noose of knowledge that there was no undo button, no way to escape her service, no way to get back any part of her. That all those options had fled, and she was trapped, trapped, trapped, and the baby sweating against her aching breast was dragging the life out of her and guzzling it down with smacking, slick lips.

She stared into the blank, black mirror of the television screen and tried out her best smile. An obviously fraudulent effort, but when Bobby stopped in the doorway to look at her, she noticed him glowing with pride and she supposed that convincing him was enough.

If everyone else believed she was happy, then sooner or later she would have to be too.

Things would get easier. They had to.

Didn't they?

CHAPTER 10

THEY DID NOT.

Three days came and went, and the breastfeeding continued to hound her. The blanket helped, and she took pleasure in knowing she was doing the best for little Bobby, but all the pride and all the blankets in the world couldn't cure the feeling of dread that thrilled through her at each needy cry as those tiny hands reached out toward her.

The first twenty-four hours are the worst. It's an adjustment phase, Jolie assured her over the phone, tinny voice pushing its way past a background bustle of running children, *but it gets easier each day.*

None of it stopped Amanda's skin from crawling when she felt that miniature mouth on her, so like his father and at the same time so different, so demanding and so strangely alien. The aching pain and emotional jolt of the let-down. The feeling of her well-earned energy being sucked out. Life was like that. Ha-ha.

Jolie may have meant well, but her prophecy proved false. Each day got harder.

She wondered, fantasized, dreamt in her few snatched moments of rest that she switched to formula, but even in the dreams she felt a twisting knot of guilt in her gut. What would Bobby think? What would Jolie say? What would Doctor A feel about it?

She wondered whether little Bobby Junior would tire of the taste.

He did not.

He was hungry all the time, seldom could be comforted without his mouth clamped around her nipple. He ate until she wept, until her skin cracked and chafed and bled and the blood mixed with the milk to form pink blotches on her breast pads. And still he guzzled, more ravenous than ever before. The tooth prodded her more and more firmly to produce, to provide, to empty herself into him. She prayed it would fall out soon.

He was growing, too.

She'd read babies lost weight during that first week, but not Bobby. Barely four days old, and he'd packed on pounds. Near enough doubled his weight, as best she could guess. His hair was feathering back in, but now it was thin and black, sprouting from his soft little skull like a weed made of wire. It reminded Amanda, when she let it, of something spidery—daddy longlegs all clustered together. Antennae. He did not take after Amanda's sunnily blonde curls, not one bit. He didn't take after his father's dull red either. She'd read their hair could change, and if the nurse said that bright tuft had fallen out, it stood to reason something entirely new could replace it again. Babies were mysteries—wasn't that what everyone said?

Hungry, hungry mysteries.

She'd tried the pump to spare herself some pain, to give herself the opportunity to catch a stretch of sleep that was more than an hour before the caterwauling prodded her back into consciousness, but it was no use. The moment she started the pump's throbbing wheeze of an engine, baby Bobby would stir and whine and cry out for her. At least, she told herself as his little mouth rooted and worked over the weary skin, he was warm and close and living. It beat some soulless plastic cups sucking on her.

And he didn't bite her too often.

She tried to remember what it was like before, but found it difficult. Like looking back on a fading dream. Three days might as well have been an eternity. She'd changed since then, she supposed. She wondered what her mom would say about that—all those Sundays spent in church learning about resurrection and transformation, but never considering that what emerged after three days might be wholly different from the person everyone knew before.

"I'm so proud of you, babe," Bobby said as they lay in bed together that third night. His arms were folded around the deflated balloon of her belly. The worst of the bleeding had stopped, but she was still throbbing between her thighs, and she still felt emptier than she ever had before. "I know this all is tough, but you're doing great. He's doing great. He'll grow up healthy and strong. Just like his mom."

"That's the goal," she said, tried to fake a smile but couldn't muster the energy. It was dark anyway. No one had to know. "It's not so bad. I can get used to it."

She wiped the clammy slick of sweat from her hands onto the sheets and wondered if he could smell her stress and prayed that he couldn't. Prayed that he wouldn't notice at all, that he would fall asleep or roll away or just take his arms off of her. The warmth of his skin was suffocating. She didn't want to be touched, didn't want to be clung to, but couldn't think of any way to fend him off without upsetting the pittance offering of rest.

Just nerves, she rehearsed, as she drifted toward sleep. A touch of anxiety. Every mother felt the same, and they all dealt with it just fine. Right? So could she. And Bobby was right—she *was* a good mom. Out-momming Jolie one hundred points to one. All those nerves and devils could go on and fuck off, she could push them out and close the door and good riddance. She was half smiling as she drifted toward sleep and a delicate, bruised part of her mind began to unclench.

But then it was night again, and the devils crept back in.

CHAPTER 11

S HE DIDN'T BOTHER checking the clock.
In the world of night, time lost all sense and purpose. Her alarm clock was a whining, hungry bellow. Each shift ended with a wet, guttural burp and sigh.

In the gaps between, quiet filtered past the blackout curtains instead of light, the edges only shifting toward pale gray after hours and hours of vigil. Bobby softly snored in the bedroom, but Amanda didn't bother going back there. It hurt too much to walk, and there was no sense in disturbing his sleep, so the bassinet sat in the corner of the den, and she huddled on the couch as far from it as she dared. A sound machine spat out its white noise blur, a constant static storm that matched her thoughts. Until the gray began to lighten the carpeting below the window, there was no time that mattered.

"The early bird gets the worm," she murmured, but she was unsure why.

Early meant nothing to the baby. Late didn't either. His mewling cries roused her from her sleep every hour, sometimes more frequently. She dozed in fits and bursts when she could, otherwise hunched in front of the television, chugging water until it spilled down her shirt and spattered her socks, anything to rehydrate, to refill, to fight back against the infant's onslaught, but it never felt like enough. The lanolin cream she dabbed onto her tortured nipples never had enough time to heal the cracked skin, had barely enough time to give even a greasy sliver of relief. The ibuprofen she devoured left a bitter chalkiness that slipped up from her stomach in ugly, stinking belches. His mouth worked while he slept, miming the process of feeding on her, that hideous tooth standing erect, a proud, tiny tower all weirdly angled and horribly out of place.

NESTING

Coffee. That's what she wanted. But coffee could make a baby sleep less, and that thought terrified her. He was draining her too quickly already. Her muscles felt weak, weaker each day, as if her body was slowly imploding, like one of those awful fruit punch pouches from children's birthday parties. Parties with the latex-condom stench of balloons and constant shrill screams. The parties she used to go to so that she could help her friends set up for their little miracles, back when the envy of their offspring sat so heavy in her throat that she could feel the bile simmering in her gullet.

She left the TV half-muted, but the quiet murmur and the glow of electric light still helped her, helped bake some part of her mind into semi-solidity. It didn't seem to bother the baby. He could sleep through or ignore just about anything except for hunger.

An animal show. Again.

She'd spent her pregnant months almost exclusively watching the daytime drama of nature—shows that inevitably featured some achingly maternal creature caring for her young to a background swell of nauseatingly optimistic music—hoping for any primal clue on what made a good mom. It was educational, she told herself. It was important.

But in the night, the shows were different. The night was the time for predators, as if whoever scheduled the shows knew that the only people awake in those lost hours were looking for something that bled.

The cheery soundtracks and pastels parted ranks and the dreadful side of nature stalked its way in. The music became an older refrain, one of bellows and pain. A lion adopted a baby deer, abducted it from its mother and dragged it off into its lair. Kept it there, offering it only meat until it starved to death, the emaciated face twisted in pitiful terror. Then the lion sought out another. And another. And another. Stressed-out mice devoured their own pink, hairless young, the tiny eyes swollen purple orbs behind lids that hadn't yet opened. A pod of orcas drowned a baby whale while the mother watched, ripped its fins off and its stomach out and left it to sink, uneaten, before they zipped off into the open water, clicking and whistling with delight while the mother mourned.

The baby fed on her, the nights distorted, and nature painted itself in warpaint red while she watched, enraptured. She knew she should doze, try to sleep, try to recover, but each moment he nursed she found herself waiting until he was done. Waiting until the next fix, when she could crowd in closer to the screen.

Other mothers watched true crime, parked their asses on the couch to hear about the husband butchering his wife in grainy, color-muted police confessionals, to see high school photos and old, overweight friends of the victim and killer alike, their faces lined from the years since the event, spectacled eyes still glinting with a hunger for fame. The crime scene photos blurred out, or black and white, or tilted at such an angle that you could see *something* terrible had happened, but not quite *what*. Just enough ugliness to hint at the loathsomeness of humanity between wine coolers and shitty paperback romances.

Amanda watched a zebra with its glistening purple intestines ripped out and fought over by two snarling wild dogs, their erections plainly visible as they shook with delight and their murdered prey feebly kicked and rolled its head from side to side in the orange dust now turning to mud. The flank muscle stretching like taffy and tearing into strips of bloody steak as they pulled apart all those beautiful stripes in the shade of some appalling, wind-bent tree.

She waited for the close-up.

By the time it came, the baby was beginning to stir again.

CHAPTER 12

MORNING ARRIVED WITH a digitized squawk from the bedroom, and then Bobby was fumbling to get dressed and packing his lunch and heading to work.

It was inevitable. He'd taken his few scraped-together vacation days, but that amounted to little more than a long weekend. Bills waited for no one. Least of all for the people who needed it the most, Amanda supposed. Bobby kissed her on the cheek and wished her well, his scarf wound around his neck and a coat so bulky around his shoulders that it made him look a bit like a balloon animal. She waved at him as he walked across the parking pad toward the little Acura, but he was turned toward the sun-glinting car and did not see her.

Alone.

She tried not to be terrified.

Not that Bobby was any great help. Sure, he changed diapers and helped comfort as best he could, but the infant's needs were remarkably narrow in scope. He ate, he slept, and occasionally gave a watery, yellow soiling that smelled only a little foul. Bobby Senior, for all his willing efforts, couldn't provide the panacea for little Bobby Junior's woes.

But Bobby-the-boyfriend offered something else, something intangible, something that she needed far more than a hand cleaning up diapers. A buzz of energy wired through her heart and fluttered against her lungs as she watched from the window.

The car pulled out and cruised off and down the road. The sky was bleak and gray, and looking at it set a chill loose across her skin. From the den, she could hear baby Bobby let out a long, trilling wail that climbed steadily in a crescendo. She shuffled her way back to check on him. She took only small steps. Half of a week had passed, but her body still felt like a porkchop that had been pulverized.

Bobby was—no surprise—red-faced and surly as he stretched like a tiny, imperious king in his bassinet throne. At the sight of her, his squealing only grew stronger until it reached an octave that she thought must be a challenge for any human being to achieve. His tooth stabbed out like a tiny bony blade. As she unbuttoned her shirt, the yowling quieted to an expectant gurgle. She scooped him up into her arms, ignoring the knifing pain in her lower back. It was hard enough to move even without a baby that felt like it was made of wet sand.

She sat down on the couch and, as practiced, slipped the baby under the blanket and up against her bare chest. Moments later she felt that little mouth clamp down around her. She flipped the television on and tried not to think about the pain. A daytime show. Still a nature documentary, but early enough that the babies-and-their-mothers circuit hadn't yet begun. This one featured some funny-looking bird called a cuckoo. She had heard of them before, but the only thing she remembered was that they popped out of clocks and that the name sounded a whole lot like kookaburras. She mumbled the kookaburra song to little baby Bobby as he gnawed on her.

> "Kookaburra sits in the old gum tree
> Eating all the gum drops he can see
> Stop, kookaburra, stop, kookaburra
> Leave some there for me."

She winced as baby Bobby gave a particularly sharp nip with his one wiggling tooth, as she felt that stinging so like a papercut, but wetter. She hoped she wasn't bleeding again. She extricated him from that nipple and guided him over to the other.

"Leave some there for me," she mumbled again in some mild attempt at levity, but the words came out humorless. She wished boyfriend Bobby were back home so fervently that a tear trickled down the edge of her nose and toward her mouth. She wiped the evidence away, focused again on the show to distract herself.

The cuckoo, the narrator confided, were generally solitary animals that fed themselves off of anything available: insects, lizards, and occasionally fruit. Most solitary birds were at a severe disadvantage when it came to the choice between defense of their nesting young and seeking out food, but not the cuckoo. The cuckoo didn't keep a home. The cuckoo was a brood parasite.

Like the cowbird, the mothers lacked any mothering skills, and instead put the burden on helpless accomplices. They'd find an appropriate host nest, lay their own egg inside it, and fly away before the mother returned. If the nest was full, the cuckoo had been known to knock eggs from the nest to make room.

A picture, then, of a shattered egg on the ground; the tiny pink bird, half-baked and beak gaping, lay like a broken toy among papery flakes of shell.

"The mothers return and take the baby as their own, feeding it and raising it. In an effort to discourage the mother from rejecting them before they can fend for themselves, cuckoo babies grow fast, demanding constant food with a rapid, begging cry," the old British voice professed.

Amanda watched, entranced, as a tiny mother bird of some diminutive species dangled and dropped a bug down into the waiting gullet of a massive, bulging cuckoo baby, easily three times as large as the would-be mother.

It was almost comical. Almost.

She realized she was drumming her fingers in a nervous tattoo against the seat cushion, and she forced herself to quit it.

"The cuckoo baby will quickly grow strong enough that the mother does not dare refuse it. And woe to those mothers who reject the intruding egg or manage to banish the fledgling invader," the narrator said. "The cuckoo mother will return and take revenge."

Another picture, another nest, but this one had been reduced to a tattered bit of brush and splintered twigs strewn across the ground. Among the broken matchsticks of the nest, egg after egg lay split and oozing yellow slime like pus. A stray feather lay beside them, sticky and red.

Her fingers were drumming again. This time she did not bother to stop.

It was trademark behavior for brood parasites, which could be found in any number of birds, fish, and even insects. Whatever other monsters joined that heinous list escaped her as she felt a sharp pull and then a looseness. The tooth that had dug into her tender, swollen flesh was suddenly moving free of its moorings and tumbling down her swollen stomach. She made a grab for it, but Bobby squirmed and then she heard a porcelain rattle as something tiny and white tumbled and bounced off the leg of the coffee table.

She let out a sigh of relief. It seemed almost too good a blessing to be true. She peeked under the blanket and past the baby's slurping lips. The offending tooth was gone, the mouth right and proper for an infant of his age. She set the blanket back in place, lest she irritate him and start him screaming again.

She craned her head to look for the tooth, but it had slipped out of sight behind the coffee table's cast-iron foot. Moving hurt far too much to make pursuit worthwhile. At least he hadn't swallowed it. She could look for it when Bobby was done feeding.

If, she thought, *not when.*

The man's words seemed to echo from moments before, and on a sudden impulse—not one of *those women*, the rational part of her mind howled—she whipped the blanket back and looked down at little baby Bobby.

Nothing.

Just the same little dark hairs, the same chubby hands and tiny toes.

Her pulse thudded, sweat trickled from her armpits, hot and slick and rank, but the baby burrowed even more uncomfortably close against her, either oblivious to the smell or—it occurred to her—enjoying it.

She wondered what she had expected to find. Maybe, she decided, she was a bit too worked up for any educational television.

She settled the blanket tent back over the feasting baby and tried to ignore the sensation of tugging while his gums bit down against her tender skin. The sudden absence of his tooth was a blessing, but not enough to make it comfortable.

It was going to be a long day. She groped around for the television remote. Maybe watching the Kardashians would help. Bobby hated the show, but with him at work, it was the perfect time to chain-watch a few episodes of mindless entertainment. All those pretty people with their unruined bodies paraded around, proud as peacocks. She left the volume down low so she could tolerate their voices.

She knew she wasn't supposed to sleep while breast feeding, but she leaned back and let her eyes drift half closed for a moment.

NESTING

Just a moment, barely a fractured sliver of rest, a chance to ease the weight from her eyes. . .
Until she felt it again.
The tooth.

CHAPTER 13

THE TOOTH.

She could feel it still there, hard and jagged against the chapped, abused skin of her areola.

Another tooth? Had there been two? That wasn't the kind of thing that just slipped by or could get filed away as postpartum forgetfulness. Maybe she simply had imagined the first falling to the ground, a product of wishful thinking and sleep deprivation?

Bobby was far too deeply involved to easily disengage, so she mustered what strength she could past the aching in her groin and pushed the coffee table back with one foot.

A monstrous weight began to throb through her heart, so close to that little suckling mite.

The tiny ivory fang was there on the floor, nesting in tangled threads of carpet. At the tooth's base, where the root should have been, a ropey black tendril protruded like a rotten stalk.

The stalk was moving.

It wiggled first one way and then another, twisting, beckoning blindly, probing clumsily along the ground as if it were some miniature disembodied finger, all slick and black and wetly shining.

That was inside my baby.

Amanda felt her battered bladder give a weak and helpless clench and then damp acid warmth was branching down her thighs. Her heart rose and fell against the anvil of her chest as she stared at the offensive growth. As she folded the absurdly cheery blanket back to look down at her precious charge.

Inside my baby.

Baby Bobby was beneath, his eyes staring up at her, wide and dark and attentive as he slurped greedily away. Amanda touched his cheek, hoping to coax a yawn out of him, but when that failed, she simply peeled his lips back to look inside.

Inside.

Milk slopped down from the corners of his mouth and he twitched in irritation. Everything looked as it should have: all pink and soft and healthy. Healthy. Toothless. But had something moved as she peeled those little lips back? What niggling tooth had scraped her?

He let out a vexed grunt as she pried his jaw wider open. A jaw, she noted, that was exceptionally strong. And there, a wriggling black finger probed up from the root of the missing tooth, a perfect twin to the hideous extension on the floor.

My baby.

He let out a squawk of distress as she shoved a thumb and two fingers past his lips, pinching and grabbing at the protrusion that slithered just out of reach. She pushed deeper. If she could just get a proper grip on it, she was sure she could pull it out. The probe slipped free with acrobatic ease and slid down into the gap his missing tooth had left.

She squeezed at his gums, some desperate hope that the pressure would force the alien stalk to appear again battling against the saner part of her mind, which moaned at her that she was being one of *those women*. That it was all in her mind and she was hurting her baby, just one more stress-crazed mouse tearing apart her young. That if she wasn't careful, she'd feel the chicken-bone pop of his jaw dislocating or his fragile skull caving in and that would be it. The end. That everything in her world was about to fall apart. The infant twisted away from her, fighting, thrusting his tongue against her hands as he began to shriek an awful, unfamiliar sort of bellow.

A sound of pain.

She scooped his tongue to the side with one hooked finger and she felt it go suddenly loose.

The tongue slipped out of the baby's mouth and landed in her lap with a moist, rubbery *PLOP!*

She stared at it for one awful moment before she could feel the teeth again, scraping across her finger. Not one, but dozens. Her breath caught and died in her throat.

His crying trailed off and struggling stilled. Those dark, alien eyes fixed upon her in silent appraisal.

Her finger tingled numbly as she stretched his mouth as wide as it could go.

The pink flesh inside was unraveling, as if that wet little tongue had been the loose end of a string and now began the great unweaving. Beneath the line of gums she could see a forest of the probes, jutting and groping. Tiny black wormy tendrils, all wiggling and prodding their jagged tips against her finger, against the soft flesh inside his mouth, in revolting contrast with that puffy little face.

She thought, suddenly, of biting into sweet fruit and finding the inside dry and dusty and caked in black mold.

Behind the rows of feelers was something worse.

Beneath where his tongue had been rooted, a pair of cleaving mandibles flexed open and shut within his plump little cheeks. Slick, ebony segments of jointed armor as thick as her thumb, ridged with bladed edges and clamping down with sharp, metallic clicks. Chewing greedily on the air as he guzzled every bit of milk he could snatch away from her.

Click. Click. Click.

Somewhere, Amanda was certain that Doctor A was gobbling her precious bloody slab of meat and clicking her approval to match.

I took your baby to the nursery myself.

We know how many we have on the unit. No babies can leave without us noticing. No patients can bring in a baby without us knowing and there's no way for them to disappear.

Except bringing one in as a doctor couldn't be too difficult, could it? Or hurriedly filling the nest herself. She had looked so disheveled when she came in for Amanda's final pushing. And there was one easy way to make the extra disappear. . .

A feeling of unprocessable horror was building up inside her chest, swelling, a massive bubble straining up her throat as it pushed toward a birthing of its own. It poured out of her mouth in a scream that strained the veins from her neck and set them quivering, that laced a memory of pressure through her hips and between her legs and deep up into her battered insides. All the while little Bobby Junior slurped away, his chin wet with her milk, his eyes ink-dark and watching, lips stretched back to reveal the mess of twitching black carapace beneath.

It wasn't until she tried to push him away that he bit down, jagged mandibles burrowing into the soft flesh of her breast.

And it wasn't until she began slapping at him, clawing furrows into that pretty pink skin, that he began to chew.

CHAPTER 14

IT WAS A solid hour before Bobby's usual quitting time for the day, and yet he found himself standing at the front door, a fistful of carnations behind his back, still swaddled in the grocery-store cellophane cone and damp from the produce mist sprayers.

He'd asked Mr. Kershel to send him home early, and for once, the old bastard hadn't given him too much trouble about it; only one long surly stare and a nearly incomprehensible mutter about how useless the youngbloods were these days.

He turned the lock and stepped inside, letting the door click shut behind him.

"Mandy? Babes?"

He stood in the foyer, rocking from foot to foot, some vague idea of pulling the flowers out and surprising her as she rushed in to greet him, bubbling over with joy. There was no answer. He supposed that his expectations might be a little high. She'd been a little weird ever since the birth, was probably asleep, certainly tired, and in no mood for surprises. The likelihood of her rushing anywhere or bubbling with anything positive was what Mr. Kershel would've called "a dry shit's chance in a warm bath."

He crept down the hallway as quietly as he could manage, toward where the television quietly muttered behind the barricade of the sofa. When he entered the den, he noticed the smell. Sharp, metallic, the kind of stench that made skin crawl, and the unmistakable scent of feces. Baby Bobby must be in dire need of a changing, he supposed, but the thought did little to drive off the instinctive unease that settled across him.

Something about the smell was wrong. Something about all of it seemed off. He should've heard her snoring. She'd snored like a drunken lumberjack at the hospital. Not cute little sighs, but great, ripping roars. Every night since then, too. And now silence.

He set the flowers on the countertop and had made it the better part of the way across the den before he passed the sofa and all thought drained from his mind.

The carpeting—picked out from Target, a white-on-yellow pattern of squares that had made Amanda coo with delight—was soaked in a cabernet red. Blood, more than he had ever imagined could exist in a person, had formed a tidal surf around the upended coffee table. Had turned to jelly on the quilt bunched up beside it. And there on the sofa, Amanda.

The mother of his child was stretched out spread-eagle, eyes bloodshot and glazed, mouth straining open, her chin and cheeks streaked with fans of crusted, scabby red.

Little else recognizable remained.

Her blouse was torn open, her chest a gaping mess. Her breasts had been removed entirely. Beneath their ragged foundation, the glistening off-white of naked bone. Her legs were spread lewdly wide, thick cotton panties on display and stained the same as the carpet. Her toes were bent and twisted from where they had struck the coffee table in wild death-throe kicks.

And there, curled up on her lap, in a pool of cooling blood, baby Bobby was sleeping soundly. His chest rose and fell with deep, contented breaths.

Bobby had his phone to his ear, 9-1-1 dialed, before he collapsed to his hands and knees and puked until bile was the only thing left, drooling from his mouth in ropey strands.

"Sir? What is the nature of your emergency?" the man on the far side of the phone asked, voice calm and a little weary.

Bobby just shook his head.

"Send someone. Send anyone," he finally managed. "She's. . ."
Murdered.

It was the only thing possible. Someone must have broken in and attacked her. It was senseless, but nothing seemed to make much sense. Animals couldn't maul her like that and then escape. The voice on the phone was talking, asking questions, but Bobby dropped it onto the blood-slicked carpet.

The baby, he thought.

Amanda seemed tragically small, disassembled, but baby Bobby looked as big as ever before. Bigger, even. He looked bloated. Another senseless thought.

He crossed the room, feet squelching across the soggy carpet and scooped little Bobby up and away from the mangled wreck of meat, lifting with both arms and hoisting the child up against him before he retreated to the far corner. He huddled down in the comforting womb of walls, staring, transfixed at her glassy eyes and contorted face.

At some point, he realized tears were streaming down his face. He stroked Bobby Junior's head and hummed a reckless, broken lullaby. Bobby Junior was heavy, far heavier than Bobby Senior had remembered. *They grow so fast.* The thought bounced around the shocked landscape of his mind, nonsensical and comfortless.

Bobby Junior nuzzled against his chest, tiny hands and mouth rooting for food.

Thwarted by the shirt, the baby began to cry.

"Shhh," Bobby said. The sound did nothing to placate the baby. "It's alright, buddy. It's going to be fine."

A lie, of course. The baby only cried louder.

He didn't know the first thing about how to quiet the kid. He had no real interest in babies, to be perfectly frank. Never had. He'd agreed to fatherhood because that was the cost of being with Amanda. Now she'd been chopped up by some psychotic and he was left huddling in the corner. He wasn't cut out for this.

The distant claxon of approaching sirens was splitting the afternoon sky when it occurred to him that the murderer might still be inside. He didn't flee. The police would be here in just a moment, and he wasn't sure he had it in himself to stand up, even if the monster who had committed the crime plopped down in front of the TV to keep up with the Kardashians. The police would know what to do.

Baby Bobby had put his tears on hold and was now chewing at his shirt, he noted. That strange little tooth snagged and tugged on the cloth. Completely oblivious to the massacre, just looking for a snack.

What would he do with a kid, now that Amanda was gone? His mind darted from topic to topic as every other bit of him turned to lead. How would he take care of the baby? He didn't know a thing about raising an infant. He'd need help.

He flinched as the baby managed to nip him through his shirt.

A mother. That's what the baby needed. Someone who could raise the child properly, even if it meant adoption.

After all, he just wasn't ready for a child of his own.

POLTERGEIST PASSWORD

NICK ROBERTS

IN THE SUMMER of 2022, all three hosts of *Broadcasts from the Grave*, a podcast focused on investigating paranormal phenomena, disappeared immediately after recording what would become their final episode. Some have speculated that the last show was a hoax itself—a fitting sendoff to a program approaching two hundred episodes devoted to supernatural occurrences. The most accepted motive for the theory was that the creators were running short of ideas and wanted to end the podcast's run on a high note.

If that were the case, then Wally Miller, Alonzo Lawrence, and Shelby Baxter, better known by their stage names, "Weird Wally," "Zombie Zo," and "Shelby Baxstabber," have all intentionally maintained a "missing person" status for over two years at the time of this documentation. Though the subjects of the later episodes gradually became more obscure compared to the widely known cryptids, hauntings, and extraterrestrial cases from the first two seasons, there remains no concrete evidence suggesting there was a plan to end the show or why the three individuals would go into hiding.

To pull off a hoax of this measure, their families—including but not limited to parents, spouses, and even young children—would have to be in on it. Again, there appears to be no financial gain, no logistical rationale for staging such a spectacle. It remains the opinion of this reporter that the content in question does in fact depict the final hours of the hosts' lives. Until proven to the contrary, by all accounts, what you are about to read is real. Provided below is the transcript of the final episode of *Broadcasts From the Grave*, titled, "Poltergeist Password."

* * *

NICK ROBERTS

A spooky theme song plays for thirty-four seconds before being lowered to background music.

WALLY
Welcome ghouls, fiends, and fellow creatures of the night to *Broadcasts From the Grave*. I'm your host, Weird Wally, joined as always by my partners in the paranormal, Mr. Zombie Zo. . .

ALONZO
What up? What up?

WALLY
And the deceptively lovely, Shelby Baxstabber.

SHELBY
Hello, lovelies.

The theme song fades out completely.

WALLY
This is episode number one-eighty-nine. Can you believe that? One-hundred and eighty-nine episodes. We are cruising right along to our bicentennial episode.

SHELBY
Amazing.

WALLY
Right? It feels like just a week ago we were brainstorming topics to cover and wondering if anyone would even listen.

ALONZO
They listened and are still listening.

POLTERGEIST PASSWORD

                    WALLY
You got that right. It's because of you,
dear morbid listener, that we are able to
keep this boat afloat. If you like what
you hear tonight and want to show your
support, giving us a simple rating and
review on whatever platform you use would
go a long way. And if you want bonus
content, you can find us on Patreon and
unlock a host of hidden horrors for just a
few dead presidents a month. Now, let's
cut to the chase and dive into the spooky
subject that is the topic of this week's
episode.

                    SHELBY
          Yes, let's do it.

                    WALLY
I know Ms. Baxstabber here is ready to
          unpack this beast.

                    SHELBY
               (laughs)
I am. I'm telling you, this one. . .this
          one is creepy.

                    ALONZO
               Hmm.

                    WALLY
Yeah, Zombie Zo, you're in for a treat
               tonight.

                    ALONZO
Well, if it scares Shelby, it's got to be
               good.

                    SHELBY
               It is.

WALLY
Listener, in case this is your first time joining us on the broadcast, it is our custom to seek out the supernatural. We scour the recesses of the internet, the dark web, and beyond, to bring you some of the weirdest, most bizarre, and sometimes downright terrifying stories, urban legends, and just all-around strange happenings and do a deep dive on the topic. Now, Shelby Baxstabber and I do our research.

SHELBY
M'hmm.

WALLY
We do the hard work and bring it all to Mr. Zombie Zo because he is your surrogate, listener. Each week, we present to him and you the facts of whatever the case may be and get his real reaction and unbiased feedback. Now, the best thing about Zo is that he is open-minded. He's not a pure skeptic, nor is he by any means a true believer in the supernatural. And that's what makes him so great. Would you say that's a fair assessment, Zo?

ALONZO
I am great. That's correct.

SHELBY
(laughs)

WALLY
Sometimes what we say shocks him. Other times, it falls flat. You never know what you're gonna get with Zombie Zo. What do

POLTERGEIST PASSWORD

you think your percentage is for believing
in some of the topics we've covered?

ALONZO
Uhh. Hmm. That's a good question.

WALLY
Thank you.

ALONZO
Well, I mean, I would say most of the
stuff y'all talk about is hard to
completely dismiss.

SHELBY
But there have been some that you straight
up laughed at.

WALLY
We won't even bring up the Winnipeg Pig
Man.

ALONZO
(laughs)
Yeah, now that one was some bullshit.

SHELBY
Aww, poor Pig Man.

ALONZO
No, for real though, the ones that get me
the most are the aliens, I think.

WALLY
I've picked up on that. Why do you think
you're more susceptible to little green
men and flying saucers than cryptids like
Bigfoot or Moth Man?

                    ALONZO
It's the statistics. We don't know if
we're alone in the universe. It's entirely
possible that there are extraterrestrial
lifeforms that've visited our planet.

                    SHELBY
            I get that.

                    WALLY
I like the way you phrased that:
"extraterrestrial lifeforms." Saying it
that way makes it more scientific than
            "aliens."

                    ALONZO
That's why I'm the voice of reason, the
        voice of the people.
            (laughs)

                    WALLY
That you are. So, are you ready to hear
what we have for you this week, Mr. Zombie
                Zo?

                    ALONZO
As my favorite vampire hunter once said,
"I was born ready, motherfucker."

                    WALLY
We'll see about that. I think we got
something that's gonna get under your skin
            tonight.

                    SHELBY
            (laughs)
        Oh, we do.

                    ALONZO
            Uh-oh.

POLTERGEIST PASSWORD

WALLY
Yeah, you brought up that you'd most
likely buy into aliens because of logic,
but what Ms. Baxstabber and I have for you
tonight is gonna play on your fears.

ALONZO
Hit me with it.

WALLY
Hit him with it, Shelby.

SHELBY
(clears throat)
Yes, will do. Mr. Zombie Zo, have you ever
heard of the Poltergeist Password?

ALONZO
The what and the what now?

WALLY
(laughs)
Oh, we got him.

ALONZO
Not some ghost shit. Y'all didn't go find
some more ghosts and demons did you? You
know I don't play like that.

WALLY
Ah ha! We know your sweet spots, sir, and
that's exactly what we did. Forget your
Ouija boards and your Bloody Marys because
we've got an urban legend that blends the
paranormal and the scientific in a way
that's gonna rattle your cage, big boy.

ALONZO
(claps and rubs hands together)
All right. I'm ready for it. Bring it on.

WALLY
Baxstabber. I believe you mentioned
something about a. . .poltergeist?

SHELBY
Indeed, I did, Wally. Indeed, I did.
(lowers voice, speaking dramatically)
For centuries, we have longed to commune
with the dead. Seances, Ouija boards,
spiritualists, mediums—these are all ways
in which mankind has tried to break
through to the spiritual realm.

ALONZO
All bullshit.

WALLY
Zo, really? I just praised your open-
mindedness, and now you've turned skeptic
on us.

ALONZO
(laughs)
Look man, if I can get it at Target, the
only ghosts it's attracting are middle-
aged white women.

SHELBY
Don't underestimate our power. We are
Legion.

WALLY
Laugh it up while you can, Zombie Zo.
That's all I can say. Let's keep your
intro going, Shelby.

SHELBY
Yes, let's. Like I was saying, as a
species, it seems like we inherently crave

POLTERGEIST PASSWORD

to connect with the dead. The most common nomenclature for a spirit in the Western world is what we refer to as a ghost.

ALONZO
Here we go.

SHELBY
But we're not talking about ghosts tonight. Tonight, it's all about poltergeists.

WALLY
Baxstabber, would you mind breaking down the difference between ghosts and poltergeists for our listeners who might be uninformed on the nuances between the two?

SHELBY
Absolutely. In the most basic terms, ghosts are visible, and poltergeists are audible.

ALONZO
So, you can't see a poltergeist?

SHELBY
There have been paranormal researchers who've used various forms of technology to capture a visual manifestation of a poltergeist, but they never appear in human form.

ALONZO
Okay. So, all the pictures of supposed spirits caught on camera are ghosts?

SHELBY
Yes. I think that's a fair assumption.

ALONZO
But what about all those floating orbs and
shit? We've done lots of episodes with
supposedly haunted places, and the people
claiming they're haunted like to use those
orbs or little lights as proof.

WALLY
I believe you're referring to spectral
energy.

ALONZO
I was just referring to floating balls,
but that sounds better.

SHELBY
Forget the pictures. They're not important
because when we think of ghosts, we
traditionally picture someone who's come
back from the dead for some reason. That's
a rabbit hole for a different episode. If
our standard ghosts can appear as
apparitions, poltergeists either can't or
don't want to be seen. But they do want to
make their presence known.

WALLY
Let me jump in for a moment with a couple
of facts that might help bring Zombie Zo
back down to ground level before we
proceed.

ALONZO
I'm ready.

WALLY
Before we get off the topic of seeing
ghosts and completely dismiss it, I'd like
to point out the severe limitations of

POLTERGEIST PASSWORD

human perception. Now, what do I mean by
that? Glad you asked. According to NASA,
Zo, *NASA*, there exists an entire
electromagnetic spectrum of light, and the
portion of that light that can be observed
by the human eye is called visible light.
Do you wanna take a guess at how much of
the spectrum we can see?

ALONZO
Hell, I don't know. . .let's go with
twenty-five percent.

WALLY
That's a respectable guess, Zombie Zo, but
it's terribly off-target, I'm sad to say.
No, the human eye can only see point-zero-
zero-three-five percent of the spectrum.

ALONZO
Damn.

WALLY
Yeah, way less than even one percent.
We're gonna let that statistic marinate
for a moment. You brought up statistics
when you were talking about the
probability of extraterrestrial life.
Really think about that. Picture yourself
in a dark room. You can't see anything,
not even your hand an inch away from your
face. You're told that you can turn the
dial on the light to point-zero-zero-
three-five percent of its capacity. How
much brighter do you think that room would
get?

ALONZO
I'm still not seeing shit.

WALLY
Correct. So, as we're sitting here in the
studio, we can look around the room and
think we're seeing everything that's here,
but we're not even seeing one percent of
what's in our presence. We could be
surrounded by ghosts and not even know it
simply because our eyes aren't
biologically designed to detect them. So,
Zombie Zo, can you give me an inch of
belief by acknowledging that it's possible
a dead woman could be standing over your
shoulder right now and you don't even know
it because of the limitations of your
perception.

ALONZO
Going off that logic, I will concede to
that possibility.

WALLY
Thank you, kind sir. And now for fact
number two. What's the first thing that
comes to mind when you hear the word
"poltergeist"?

ALONZO
The movie.

WALLY
Of course. I would agree and say that most
people only know the term "poltergeist"
because of the classic 1982 film directed
by Tobe Hooper.

SHELBY
That's where I learned it. God, that movie
scared me as a kid. "They're here."

POLTERGEIST PASSWORD

ALONZO
Yep. The little girl talking to the TV,
shit flying everywhere. But it was that
damn clown scene that got me.

WALLY
I'm glad you brought up "shit flying
everywhere." We'll get back to that in a
minute, but first I want to define our
terms, if you will. "Poltergeist" is a
German word. *Poltern* means to "make
sound," and *geist* means "ghost or spirit."
Add them together and it roughly
translates to "noisy ghost."

ALONZO
But I thought she said poltergeists
weren't ghosts?

SHELBY
Think of poltergeists as a sub-genre of
ghosts. Not all ghosts are poltergeists,
but all poltergeists are ghosts.
Poltergeists have been compared to angry
children. They lash out by making noises
or moving objects that we can detect in
our plane of existence. There was a lot of
that in the movie.

ALONZO
Okay. Okay. I'm following.

WALLY
If we add up everything we've discussed so
far, then it's possible for poltergeists
to exist beyond the limits of human
perception, and they distinguish
themselves from apparitions because they
aren't trying to be seen, only to get
attention or cause chaos. We don't know

the exact reason for their antics, hence the angry child comparison.

ALONZO
This is interesting. I feel like I'm getting a crash course on spirits right now, and I'm digging it. I'm eagerly awaiting to see where this is headed.

SHELBY
It's headed to the Poltergeist Password.

ALONZO
And what is the Poltergeist Password?

WALLY
The Poltergeist Password is. . .something that we'll learn about after this brief break from our sponsor.

ALONZO
Ah, hell.

The spooky theme song plays underneath the following advertisement read.

SHELBY
(mock announcer voice)
Who doesn't need to scare up their closet? If you're anything like me, then you are always on the hunt for the latest and greatest spooky merch. Sure, everyone has shirts, hats, hoodies, coffee mugs—all a dime a dozen. What you really need are high-quality, hand-spun cotton socks that will terrify your toes. Yes, Spooky Socks features high-quality, officially licensed horror footwear, ranging in everything from the classic Universal monsters like Dracula, Frankenstein's monster, and the

POLTERGEIST PASSWORD

Wolfman to the new wave of seventies horror like *The Exorcist* and *Jaws*, and everyone's favorite line of slashers like Michael, Freddy, Jason, Leatherface, Chucky, just to name a few. They've even got elevated socks to match your elevated horror like *The VVitch, Hereditary,* and *Get Out.* If you want to bring some horror to your drawer, then look no further than Spooky Socks. And don't forget to use the code: BROADCASTS FROM THE GRAVE to get an additional ten percent off your entire order. You heard that right folks, forget those cheap knock-off socks with printed-on designs and get some high-quality footwear with as much grip as the monster under the bed eyeballing your exposed feet. Scare it and everyone else off with a fresh new pair of Spooky Socks. And now, Weird Wally, back to you.

Spooky theme song fades out.

WALLY
Gosh, you're good at that, Baxstabber. I know you're rocking a pair of Spooky Socks right now. Wanna tell the listeners what you got and make 'em jealous?

SHELBY
Oh, these?

ALONZO
Hey-o, you better keep those legs under the table or you're gonna be raising more than just the dead.

WALLY
What do you have on over there?

NICK ROBERTS

SHELBY
Well, these are my officially licensed
Longlegs socks.

WALLY
I see they live up to their namesake
because they're riding all the way up to
your knee. I don't think I'm speaking out
of school here when I say that I think
Nicolas Cage would approve.

ALONZO
Oh, don't even get me started on that
fuckin' movie.

SHELBY
Hey!

WALLY
Blasphemy, Zombie Zo, blasphemy.

ALONZO
What? It was weird, and it had no idea
what movie it wanted to be.

WALLY
Don't worry. We'll make a proper film buff
out of you yet. Apologies to the legions
of listeners who actually do have good
taste in movies and were morally outraged
by my co-host's inexcusable outburst.

ALONZO
(laughs)
Yeah, okay. So, are you gonna get to this
Poltergeist Password thing tonight or
what? I'm getting a little bored over
here. I think it's that time of the show,
if you know what I mean.

POLTERGEIST PASSWORD

SHELBY
I think Zombie Zo wants me to break out
this episode's drink, Wally.

WALLY
You know what? I think that's a wonderful
idea. Ms. Baxstabber, why don't you
introduce your latest creepy concoction,
and I'll get them prepped while you're
talking.

*Muffled noises as Wally presumably gets
out of his chair and starts making drinks.
Glasses clink, bottle caps twist open, and
liquid pours in the background.*

ALONZO
Okay, so what kind of drink are we working
with tonight?

SHELBY
What we have tonight is none other than
Poltergeist Punch.

ALONZO
Oooh, tell me more.

SHELBY
To summon the spirits—both kinds—we're
using Green Berry Rush Hawaiian Punch,
with a splash of SKYY Vodka, and an extra
special, special ingredient.

WALLY
(off mic)
Extra special, indeed.

ALONZO
Now wait a minute. I don't care how much I

love you guys. . .I don't drink anything unless I know exactly what's in it.

SHELBY
Uh oh, did big bad Mr. Zombie Zo have a traumatic experience in college?

ALONZO
(laughs)
Many, but not because someone spiked my drink. Seriously, what's going into those glasses, Wally?

Movement and shuffling around as Wally sits back down and distributes the drinks in what sounds like glass tumblers by the way he places them on the table.

WALLY
(settling back in and adjusting his mic)
Okay, everyone got their drinks?

SHELBY
Yep.

ALONZO
Yeah, I've got this mystery drink.

WALLY
Oh, it's not a mystery yet, Zombie Zo. That's just punch and vodka. The mystery has yet to be revealed.

ALONZO
I'm all ears.

WALLY
(in a dramatic tone)
And now, dear listeners, is when we start to take things a bit more seriously. Yes,

POLTERGEIST PASSWORD

we've got our weekly drinks that've become
fan favorites—

SHELBY
And we're so grateful for everyone who
comments what they think of them. Please
keep commenting and recommending. Every
bit helps!

WALLY
We definitely appreciate your feedback as
I've previously stated how much it helps
this little podcast of ours. But we must
get on with the show. We have much to
discuss and even more to. . .experience.

ALONZO
I don't like the sound of that.

WALLY
Just hold on to your britches, Zombie Zo,
because if the legends surrounding the
Poltergeist Password are true, we're all
in for one helluva show.

ALONZO
Alright, you've been teasing it long
enough. The listeners are still tuned in;
I guarantee it. You've got us hooked. Now
move along.

SHELBY
We've gotta keep them in suspense for as
long as possible. Every master storyteller
knows that.

ALONZO
Get to it, or I'm downing my drink and
calling for seconds.

WALLY
(laughs)
You're right. It's time to get to it.
According to legend, there exists a way of
not only summoning poltergeists but making
them visible. This method is called the
Poltergeist Password, and we're going to
do it tonight. Right now. What do you
think about that, Zombie Zo?

ALONZO
I'm intrigued. I think we're all gonna end
up drunk and slurring through the second
half of the show, but that's your all's
purview.

WALLY
In researching the Poltergeist Password
legend, I started with Wikipedia. I
followed the links to a few blogs where
people had talked about it, but no one
actually knew what it was, let alone tried
it. I jumped on Reddit, and that's when
the white rabbits on the discussion boards
took me even further down the rabbit hole.
Everyone seemed to know someone who knew
someone who had tried it, but I couldn't
track down a primary source. Which, if you
buy into the legend, there wouldn't be a
living primary source.

ALONZO
Hold up. So, you got us trying out
something like *Candyman*?

WALLY
Well, I guess that depends. What do you
mean by that?

POLTERGEIST PASSWORD

SHELBY
I think he's saying there's no real win
with *Candyman* because if he doesn't appear
when you say his name five times, then
it's just another spooky story, but if he
does, you're fucking dead.

ALONZO
See! She gets it.

WALLY
Hey, hey. There's a silver lining to this
one that's different than *Candyman*. You
have to get a little drunk to do it.

ALONZO
(laughs)
Okay. Okay. Continue.

WALLY
Ladies and gentlemen, boys and girls,
night creatures of all ages, what I'm
about to present to you came at somewhat
of a great cost and many hours of
research. I would like to introduce to the
creepy court, Exhibit A.

Six seconds of dead air ensue.

ALONZO
What the hell is that?

SHELBY
Oh, that's so rad. I've been waiting to
see it in person myself, Zo.

WALLY
This little vial, my friends, is how we
get the Poltergeist Password.

ALONZO
It looks like a mini liquor bottle.

WALLY
After scouring the recesses of the Dark
Web, I found someone. Someone who claimed
to be the younger sibling of a victim of
the Poltergeist Password.

ALONZO
Hold up. You bought some shit off the Dark
Web?

WALLY
I won't give out the young lady's username
here for obvious reasons, but she claimed
that her older brother had heard about the
legend and wanted to try it out with his
friends. He tracked down the vial like I
did and tested it out.

ALONZO
So, how does it work? You just drink it?

WALLY
You're halfway there, my friend. No,
that's just part of the puzzle. No one
knows for sure what's in this little
concoction or who discovered or made it.
Some people speculate it's nothing more
than a type of alcohol with hallucinogenic
properties similar to absinthe, while
others claim it's cursed holy water, the
type of stuff used at black mass rituals.

ALONZO
I'm about to tap out already.

WALLY
Hang on there, brother. Let me finish. So,

POLTERGEIST PASSWORD

this guy who gets the bottle—the older
brother of the woman I bought it from—he
takes a drop because that's all you're
supposed to take. That's another part of
the lore that if you take more than a
drop, it could be fatal, turning you into
a poltergeist yourself.

SHELBY
I already know all this, and I'm getting
creeped out hearing you say it. It just
feels more real now.

WALLY
No, no. You can't chicken out on me. I
haven't even gotten to the good stuff yet.

ALONZO
Well, if we're going to poison ourselves,
I can't wait for the grand finale.

WALLY
(laughs)
So, after you take your drop, you peel
back the label. Here look at it.

ALONZO
What is that? Oh, it looks like somebody
just wrapped tape around the bottle. Like
a bandage or something. Shelby, check this
out.

SHELBY
Weird. I wonder how much you have to
unwrap. . .

ALONZO
Unwrap for what? Why are we peeling back
the label?

WALLY
Like I was saying, once you peel back the label, and judging by the little perforations here, it looks like you just tear off about a half inch, it'll break free. But once you tear off your piece, it becomes *your* piece.

ALONZO
What's that supposed to mean?

WALLY
Only you can see the word on it. And the word only appears after you've taken a drop.

ALONZO
Yooo, what the fuck.
(laughs)
Here we go with the creepy shit. Sorry, please, continue.

WALLY
You can probably guess where this is headed by now, but once you see the word, you say it out loud ten times.

ALONZO
Oh, so the poltergeists are bigger and badder than Beetlejuice, Candyman, and Bloody Mary put together.

WALLY
I didn't come up with the rules. I'm just the messenger. And researcher. And dark web aficionado, apparently.

SHELBY
And now for the best part.

POLTERGEIST PASSWORD

ALONZO
Huh?

SHELBY
Don't you wanna know what happens after
you say your word ten times?

ALONZO
I don't know. Do I?
(laughs)

WALLY
This is where more of the "science" kicks
in. And, yes, I'm putting "science" in air
quotes. Whatever is in that bottle
interacts with your word to produce—hang
on, let me read my notes verbatim—it uses
kinetic energy to not only attract
poltergeists but also makes them
temporarily visible.

ALONZO
Alright, so we're ringing the dinner bell
for a bunch of damn poltergeists now, are
we? What are we supposed to do when they
show up? What's the payoff?

WALLY
That is a damn good question, Zombie Zo.
What's the point in us seeing something
supernatural on a podcast? I have two
answers to that. First, we've got our
phones. If these chaotic little critters
do in fact show up, we're going to catch
them on camera.

ALONZO
How do we do that? And since when did this
podcast start using video?

NICK ROBERTS

SHELBY
Once Wally heard about the legend and
actually got the vial from the internet,
he splurged a little bit on some new
hardware.

ALONZO
Where is it?

WALLY
There's a mini cam sitting right on top of
that computer tower in the corner.

ALONZO
Well, I'll be damned. Have you been
recording the whole time?

WALLY
No. We'll turn it on once we start the
ritual. I think it's a good time to
describe our studio setup, especially if
you're a first-time listener. Our little
makeshift studio is a room in my house. We
did some soundproofing to the walls,
plopped a table right down in the middle
here, and we all sit around it with our
headsets. Our Patreon subscribers have
seen pictures of it on the main feed.
That's one reason why you should join the
Broadcasts From the Grave Patreon, but
here's another. Any visuals, whether they
be video or pictures, we'll upload to
Patreon exclusively. By the time this
episode goes live, all the camera footage
will have been already linked and ready
for consumption, assuming we catch
anything, of course.

*Reporter's note: No video evidence was recovered from Wally's
home studio, nor discovered at Alonzo and Shelby's separate

POLTERGEIST PASSWORD

residences. Though, as you will notice in this transcript, the hosts did attempt to utilize the camera and their phones. Or, if you believe this was a hoax, then it was all theater of the mind, an audio illusion pulled off by amateur actors who continue to play their roles as missing persons at the time of this writing. In any case, no such camera or cell phones were left behind. According to the case file this reporter obtained, WALLY's home, as vandalized and damaged as it was upon discovery, yielded no evidence to support the events that transpired on the remainder of the episode. Again, the only glimpse into what really happened that night lies within the final episode itself.

                    ALONZO
          What's the second part?

                    WALLY
          Second part to what?

                    ALONZO
     You said you have two answers to my
     question about what the payoff was if—

                    WALLY
     Ah, yes. The second reason for summoning
      the potential poltergeists is that you,
     dear listener, get to hear our responses.
     I promise you, once we begin the ritual, I
      will leave the remainder of the episode
      unedited. In case you're wondering, our
     episodes typically run well over an hour.
     We do our best to trim here and there to
     bring the runtime to just under an hour.
       Most of the cuts are from unnecessary
        sounds that no one needs to hear and
     digressions or tangents we're all guilty
                    of going on.

                    SHELBY
     Are you admitting that you edit out all of
               Zombie Zo's farts?

WALLY
It's a rough job, but someone has to do
it.

ALONZO
I'm not the chief noisemaker, miss coughs-
a-lot.

SHELBY
I can't help it if my throat gets dry.

WALLY
Oh, don't worry. I cut all those
out. . .and your loud gulps.

SHELBY
I am not a loud drinker.

WALLY
See, this is a digression, dear listener,
that's a prime example of something that
will be cut from the final edit. Or I
might leave it in. It could show the
audience how much work I put into making
this production sound professional.

ALONZO
Leave it. People love behind-the-scenes
content.

WALLY
That is a fact. Speaking of behind-the-
scenes content, Miss Baxstabber, would you
mind cueing up the camera?

SHELBY
Got it.

POLTERGEIST PASSWORD

Sounds of a chair scooting and footsteps as Shelby presumably walks to the camera and turns it on.

                    SHELBY
                   (off mic)
               We are rolling.

                    WALLY
Excellent. Okay, let's right this ship and
get back to the task at hand: seeing if
there's any merit in the legend of the
Poltergeist Password. Sitting in front of
the three of us is this episode's themed
drink, but the Hawaiian punch and vodka in
our glasses is moot without a drop from
this little baby.

                    ALONZO
I still can't believe we're gonna drink
something from a vial you bought off the
dark web.

                    WALLY
Just go with it, brother. I will begin by
putting one drop in my drink. Here we go.
Okay, listeners, I have administered the
single drop, and now I must peel back my
piece of parchment wrapped around this
bottle. I won't look at it yet. Got it.
I'm placing the strip of paper face down
on the studio table and handing the vial
to Ms. Baxstabber now.

                    SHELBY
Thank you. Wow, this thing is heavier than
it looks.

                    WALLY
My thoughts exactly.

SHELBY
It must be because of the paper wrapped around it. It's so tight. Okay, I'm taking off the lid and putting my drop in my drink. There's no detectible odor to the liquid. It's clear but thick like cough syrup.

ALONZO
It's some kind of syrup, alright. Something that's probably gonna make us trip balls and have a full-blown meltdown on air.

WALLY
Hey, that would be interesting, too.

SHELBY
I am now carefully tearing off my piece of paper. As badly as I want to turn it over to see if there's anything written on it, I will avoid temptation out of respect to the ritual.

WALLY
That's the spirit.

SHELBY
Here you go, Zombie Zo. It's all yours.

ALONZO
Greeaat. Okay. Damn this fucker is heavy.

WALLY
(laughs)
Why are you holding it up to the light?

ALONZO
To try and see what's in it. See if there's any particles floating around.

POLTERGEIST PASSWORD

SHELBY
You know, for such a big man, you sure do
scare easy.

ALONZO
There's a fine line between scared and
smart. And don't you come at me like that,
Ms. *Baxstabber.*

SHELBY
(laughs)
I kid.

WALLY
Come on now. Let's get this show on the
road.

ALONZO
I'm just building suspense for the
listeners. Don't you know anything about
podcasting?

WALLY
Everything I learned about hosting a show,
I learned from Howard Stern, and that man
knows how to keep an audience on the edge
of their seats. You staring at a bottle
and giving us nothing but dead air is not
the most compelling content.

ALONZO
Well, you're a good editor, remember?

WALLY
Dear listener, if something happens to Mr.
Zombie Zo during this podcast, hopefully
you'll understand my motives and see my
actions as completely justifiable.

ALONZO
(laughs)
I hear you. Alright, I'm adding a drop to
my drink now.

SHELBY
Careful not to spill it and add too much.
No pressure.

ALONZO
There we go. My drink has officially been
spiked, and I'm ready to see some fuckin'
ghosts now.

WALLY
That's the spirit!

SHELBY
No pun intended.

WALLY
How dare you? All of my puns are intended.
Mr. Zombie Zo, I'm afraid you forgot a
step.

ALONZO
What are you talking about now?

SHELBY
The word. The paper. Tear it off.

ALONZO
Oh yeah. Okay, I just put the lid back on
the bottle, and I'm unwrapping my piece of
paper. There. And just like my cohosts, my
paper is now face down on the table. Here
you go, Weirdo. Take your cursed vial of
dark web bile back to the crackhead who
sold it to you.

POLTERGEIST PASSWORD

WALLY
Thank you, sir. How's everyone feeling?

SHELBY
I'm a little nervous. I'm not gonna lie.

ALONZO
Yeah, I'm not trying to play cool. This is
freaking me out a bit. Not the paranormal
stuff, just the fact that I could drink
this and wake up in a bathtub full of ice,
missing a few organs.

WALLY
Gang, that's what makes this episode
unique. I'd be lying if I said I wasn't
feeling a little apprehensive myself. But
a better man than me once said that
everything you want is on the other side
of fear, so let's do this. I'll go first.

ALONZO
Here we go.

WALLY
Listeners, I've got my glass in hand, and
now it goes down the hatch.

*Wally gulps and the sound of glass hitting
the table can be heard.*

WALLY
Ahhh.

ALONZO
How was it?

SHELBY
No, read the word, the word.

NICK ROBERTS

ALONZO
Oh yeah, read that shit. You're supposed
to do it real quick, right?

Sounds of paper crinkling.

WALLY
You. You. You. You. You. You. You. You.
You. You.

ALONZO
What the hell was that?

SHELBY
Was that your word?

WALLY
Yeah. Look.

ALONZO
There's nothing on your paper, man. Quit
fuckin' around.

WALLY
What? What the fuck? It said YOU just a
second ago. I'm not kidding.

SHELBY
Are you being for real right now?

WALLY
Yes! It's fucking blank now.

SHELBY
The legend said that only you can see the
word. This is crazy.

WALLY
Well, somebody go next. Let's see if it
happens again.

POLTERGEIST PASSWORD

ALONZO
Do you feel any different?

WALLY
I mean, I feel like I just had a shot of
vodka, but no, I don't feel unusual. I
cannot believe this paper is blank.

SHELBY
One, two, three.

Shelby gulps and the glass hits the table.

SHELBY
(coughs)

WALLY
Quick, read the paper.

SHELBY
(coughs again and grunts in disgust)
Are. Are. Are. Are. Are. Are. Are. Are.
Are. Are.

ALONZO
What'd it tell you to do? Act like a
goddamn a seal?

SHELBY
My word was ARE.

ALONZO
A-R-E?

SHELBY
How else would you spell it?

ALONZO
I didn't know if you meant the word or
just the letter.

WALLY
You feel okay, Shelby?

SHELBY
Yeah. That was a strong drink, and it went
down the wrong hole at the end there. But
yeah, I feel fine.

ALONZO
Oh shit, look at your word.

Sounds of shuffling and fumbling paper.

SHELBY
Holy fuck!

WALLY
Show us.

ALONZO
Are you kidding me? I gotta see this for
myself.

WALLY
Listeners, Ms. Baxstabber's paper is as
blank as mine. It appears that the words
are disappearing after we read them. And
now Mr. Zombie Zo is preparing himself for
his drink. Okay, he's picked it up.

ALONZO
The running commentary doesn't help.

WALLY
Well then quit piddling around and down
that thing.

ALONZO
Fuck it.

POLTERGEIST PASSWORD

Alonzo gulps and the glass hits the table.

                    ALONZO
                   (hisses)

                    SHELBY
Do your word. Don't say anything yet. Just
            read your word.

                    ALONZO
                   (laughs)

                    WALLY
Quit stalling and read it. What are you
                  doing?

                    ALONZO
Fucked. Fucked. Fucked. Fucked. Fucked.
Fucked. Fucked. Fucked. Fucked. Fucked.

                    SHELBY
Your word was FUCKED?

                    ALONZO
You gotta see it to believe it.

                    WALLY
It's blank, too.

                    ALONZO
What the fuck. You all are putting me on,
right? This is some disappearing ink or
       some shit. Has to be.

                    WALLY
Maybe there's some kind of activator on
the paper that causes the word to appear
when it's peeled and then disappear.

ALONZO
Yeah, like disappearing ink.

SHELBY
This is so weird.

ALONZO
Hold up.
(laughs)
You clowns think you're funny.

WALLY
We have to be for the show, of course, but
what do you mean?

ALONZO
You are fucked.

WALLY
Is that a threat Zombie Zo?

SHELBY
Holy shit. The words!

ALONZO
Exactly. You all think you're funny.

WALLY
What am I missing, guys? Help me out.

ALONZO
Are you going for an Academy Award right
now or something because I don't think
they give those out to podcast hosts. If
you put all three of our words together,
what does it say?

WALLY
"You. . .are. . .fucked." Holy shit.

POLTERGEIST PASSWORD

ALONZO
Don't act like y'all didn't set this up.

SHELBY
I swear to God I had nothing to do with
this.

WALLY
Don't look at me, man. All I did was buy
the thing.

ALONZO
You're telling me you didn't rig this word
thing?

WALLY
No! Seriously. I didn't fool around with
it until tonight. I purposefully kept it
tucked away because I wanted my first
reaction to be live on the show.

SHELBY
Did you find anything in your research
about the words spelling out a phrase like
that? I didn't.

WALLY
No.

ALONZO
Okay, okay. Assuming y'all are telling the
truth, and I'm choosing to believe you
are, then this thing could easily be
rigged.

WALLY
I agree. It could have words that make
phrases. And it could have disappearing
ink.

SHELBY
Yeah, but what gets me is the number.

WALLY
What do you mean?

SHELBY
There are three of us. It gave us a three-
word sentence. Like, how would it know
that?

WALLY
That's tricky. I'm sure it can be done. I
need to do more research on it. This might
be our first ever two-part episode,
listeners.

ALONZO
Putting all that aside, what's supposed to
happen now? We did everything, right?

SHELBY
We did.

WALLY
And now, listeners, we wait. According to
the legend, we basically just shot a
signal flare into the spiritual realm. I'm
not sure of how long it's supposed to
take, but we should experience paranormal
phenomena typically associated with
poltergeists.

SHELBY
Plus, we're supposed to see them.

WALLY
Yes, good point, Ms. Baxstabber. The drop
of this mysterious elixir supposedly
broadens our perception of the visible

POLTERGEIST PASSWORD

light spectrum. It supersizes our eyes'
ability to process vibrational
wavelengths.

ALONZO
I love it when you get all scientific on
me.

WALLY
Tone it down, Zombie Zo. This isn't that
type of broadcast.

ALONZO
(laughs)
Oh shit. Hold up.

WALLY
What's wrong? Do you sense something?

ALONZO
No, but didn't you say that poltergeists
are different than regular ghosts because
they don't want to be seen?

SHELBY
Correct. The research I did pretty much
said that they want to be noticed, not
necessarily "seen," though.

WALLY
What's the matter, Zo? Are you afraid
we're gonna piss them off?

ALONZO
Uh. . .yeah.

SHELBY
It does seem a little invasive now that I
think about it.

NICK ROBERTS

WALLY
Elaborate, please.

SHELBY
We're calling them here and then forcing
them to be seen.

ALONZO
For real. If I was just chillin' in my
little ghost realm and all of a sudden I
get yanked into a recording studio butt
ass naked, I might not take too kindly to
that.

WALLY
We should be so lucky. Not only would we
show that the legend is true, but we'd
have it captured on video and audio. Our
listenership would skyrocket.

SHELBY
You should probably trim that last line
out.

WALLY
I could. It does make me seem biased and
motivated by financial gain, but keep in
mind, we are recording on video right now.
Any cuts or edits could damage the
credibility of the show. I want this all
to be one continuous shot. I don't want
there to be any room for people to say
anything was rigged or it's special
effects or AI or any of that.

ALONZO
Don't be naïve, brother. With today's
technology, anything can be augmented.
Seeing is no longer believing for me.

POLTERGEIST PASSWORD

SHELBY
I agree. I've seen too many deep fakes to
believe anything I see. I hate to be that
cynical, but it's true.

WALLY
I appreciate your all's concerns, but I
remain optimistic and have faith in you,
dear listener, that you will take our word
for it that everything you experience on
our podcast is one hundred percent
genuine. Besides, if we had the budget for
convincing special effects, I would've
rigged the game many episodes ago.
(laughs)
Kidding, only kidding.

ALONZO
Shelby, you keep looking around the room.
You curious?

SHELBY
(laughs)
I gotta admit that yeah, I am.

WALLY
I'm sorry to do this to you, listeners,
but it is that time in the show to pay the
bills, and that means we have another word
from our sponsor.

ALONZO
(laughs)
Aww, you're cruel.

WALLY
What? You want to keep getting paid,
right?

SHELBY
I do. And I want to keep getting free
merch. People love my *Bride of Chucky*
socks.

Spooky music begins to play.

WALLY
You just heard it from a customer. People
love Spooky Socks. I know I do. Spooky
Socks is the premier company for not just
quality footwear but expertly designed
horror icons and iconography that'll turn
heads no matter where you go. Founded only
two years ago by one of Hollywood's
leading special effects creators, Spooky
Socks has only skyrocketed in popularity
since their first pair hit the shelves. In
fact—

SHELBY
Hey, sorry. Did you hear that?

WALLY
Hang on, Shelb. I'm almost finished with
the ad read.

ALONZO
No, seriously. I heard it, too.

The spooky theme music abruptly cuts off.

WALLY
Okay. I'll redo the ad read later. What
did you all hear? You're both looking up.

SHELBY
That's because it sounded like it was
upstairs.

POLTERGEIST PASSWORD

ALONZO
Not just upstairs. Like something hit the
roof. That's what it sounded like to me,
at least.

WALLY
Dear listeners, as I've explained before,
we record this broadcast from my home
studio on the first floor of a two-story
house. Zombie Zo claims to have just heard
something strike my roof.

ALONZO
I don't *think*. I definitely heard
something.

WALLY
Okay. I didn't hear anything, and this is
my house. I'm used to every sound this
place makes. I can hear your all's car
doors close from inside the kitchen. If
something hit my roof, I think I'd know.

SHELBY
There! It just happened again. Did you
hear it?

ALONZO
Wally, you heard that, right?

WALLY
I, uh. . .I did hear something that time.

ALONZO
Yeah, you were too caught up in the word
from our sponsor the first time. What was
it? Have you heard that before?

WALLY
No. Holy shit! It sounds like someone's

throwing rocks or something on the roof. It's definitely coming from the roof. I really hope our mics are picking this up.

No noises other than the host's reactions can be heard on the recording.

                    SHELBY
        Wait, listen. Do you hear how hard the
                 wind is blowing?

                    WALLY
                  Holy shit.

The apparent sound of thunder booming can be heard in the distance.

                    WALLY
        Damn, I didn't know it was supposed to
                 storm tonight.

                   ALONZO
            Whoa! What was that?

                   SHELBY
          Sounded like a tree branch.

There's a commotion like Wally taking off his headphones and scooting his seat over and footsteps across the room. A door opens.

                    WALLY
                  (off mic)
        I'm looking through the kitchen window.
        It's blowing dead branches off the trees.
        I knew I should've gotten those old things
                cut down last summer.

POLTERGEIST PASSWORD

ALONZO
Jesus! It sounded like a big one just hit
your roof.

WALLY
(off mic)
Yep. That's exactly what it is.

SHELBY
Those trees aren't gonna come crashing
through your house, right?

WALLY
(off mic)
No guarantees.

SHELBY
Greeaaat.

WALLY
(off mic)
Looks like it's dying down a bit. Damn
that was one hell of a gust.

ALONZO
Sounds like pebbles or little branches are
still hitting your roof.

WALLY
(off mic)
Yeah.

SHELBY
Come get back on mic, Wally.

*Sounds of Wally shutting the door, walking
across the room, and putting his headphones
back on.*

WALLY
(resuming his dramatic voice)
Weird Wally here, dear listeners, and we've just experienced the first disturbance of the night after having performed the Poltergeist Password ritual.

ALONZO
(laughs)
Oh, come on. That was wind. It's just a storm blowing through.

WALLY
That's a big "just" in your statement, Zombie Zo. I don't think I'm jumping to any outlandish conclusions in pointing out that it started to storm as soon as we finished the ritual.

ALONZO
That it did, but as of right now, it's a correlation and not a causation.

SHELBY
Ohh, I love it when you put that doctorate of yours to use.

ALONZO
(laughs)
I'm sitting in Wally's old office doing a podcast; it's not exactly what I had in mind as a post-grad plan.

WALLY
Dear listener, take no offense to the dismissive tone in which Mr. Zombie Zo referred to *Broadcasts From the Grave's* home base studio. I'm sure he wasn't trying to be rude. It's just that we sometimes pale in comparison to his intellectual prowess.

POLTERGEIST PASSWORD

                    ALONZO
                   (laughs)
Cut that shit out, man. Oh, I need another
                    drink.

                    SHELBY
I think that sounds like a lovely idea. No
more weird drops though. Weird Wally,
             would you like one?

                    WALLY
Sure, why not? We've got nothing but time
as we wait to witness any more strange
occurrences or coincidences, as Zombie Zo
             would have me say.

                    ALONZO
     I'm just keeping you honest.

                    WALLY
How dare you, sir? But I appreciate the
     intent. You ground us with your
credibility and accountability. What would
           we do without you?

                    SHELBY
                  (off mic)
I can detect the bullshit in your tone
            from over here.

                    ALONZO
                   (laughs)
        Y'all are too much.

A loud sound of breaking glass.

                    SHELBY
             (shrieks off mic)

WALLY
What the hell was that?

SHELBY
(off mic)
The fucking glass just exploded in my
hand!

ALONZO
Are you okay, Shelb?

SHELBY
(off mic)
No! I'm covered in fucking Hawaiian Punch
and vodka and glass. Look!

WALLY
Are you hurt?

SHELBY
(off mic)
I don't think so.

WALLY
Zo, will you run to the kitchen and grab
some paper towels.

ALONZO
Will do. Shelb, you sure you're not cut or
anything?

SHELBY
I'm fine. Fucking shit just scared me.
(laughs)
Did either of you see that?

Sounds of Alonzo taking off his headset and placing it on the table. He scoots his chair out.

POLTERGEIST PASSWORD

ALONZO
(off mic)
I didn't see what happened, but I heard
it, and it sounded like a goddamn
explosion. Not natural.

WALLY
Listener, what you just heard could be our
second occurrence of something
unexplainable since uttering the infamous
Poltergeist Password.

SHELBY
(off mic)
For real!

WALLY
Ms. Baxstabber seems to be more of a
believer or at least open-minded than she
appeared at the beginning of this
broadcast.

SHELBY
(off mic)
It literally exploded in my hand.

WALLY
Can you lean into the mic and say that
again, please?

SHELBY
I went to grab the glass, and it literally
exploded in my hand.

WALLY
Yet, your hand is not bleeding, correct?

SHELBY
No.

NICK ROBERTS

WALLY
Interesting.

Sounds of footsteps as Alonzo enters the studio.

ALONZO
(off mic)
Here you go. Damn, that is a mess. There's glass and shit all over the place over here.

WALLY
Just throw a towel on it after Shelby's finished. I'll clean it up after the show. The video is still rolling, and I don't want to edit all this out.

Footsteps as Alonzo approaches his chair and puts on his headphones.

ALONZO
You said the video. We need to watch that shit.

SHELBY
(off mic)
It didn't pick up anything. I was standing right here beside the table when it happened. The camera was pointing straight at you guys.

WALLY
Damnit. Well, at least we've got audio, and if you've listened to any of our previous broadcasts, then you know that Ms. Baxstabber—consummate host and professional as she may be—is no Meryl Streep.

POLTERGEIST PASSWORD

SHELBY
(off mic)
Hey! What's that supposed to mean?

ALONZO
(laughs)
You dry, Shelb, or do you need more?

SHELBY
(off mic)
I'm good. Thank *you*, Zombie Zo, for
asking.

WALLY
Hey! I'm the one who told him to get the
towels.

SHELBY
(off mic)
You just called me a bad actress.

WALLY
(laughs)
I love ya, but that reaction was genuine.
You couldn't have faked it.

*Sounds of Shelby moving things around and
walking to her chair.*

ALONZO
Careful now. Watch out for glass.

*She pulls out her chair and puts on her
headphones.*

WALLY
Okay, Mr. Zombie Zo, what do you make of
what's happened so far? I guess I should
say Dr. Zo, since I'm asking for your
expert opinion.

NICK ROBERTS

                    ALONZO
      I think we've just experienced two
                  coincidences.

                    WALLY
           And how can you be so sure?

                    ALONZO
      The Poltergeist Password did two things,
                    right?

                    WALLY
      Ahh, I see where you're going with this. I
               admire your logic.

                    ALONZO
      First, it attracts the poltergeists. . .

                    WALLY
         And then you see them. That's a fair
      point. Ms. Baxstabber, what do you think?

                    SHELBY
      I think urban legends in general are just
        morbid versions of the telephone game.

                    ALONZO
                Telephone game?

                    SHELBY
        Yeah, you never played that in grade
        school? You sit in a circle with your
      friends and whisper something to someone,
      and they have to repeat it to the person
       beside them, and so on and on until it
       gets all the way back around the circle.
       Most of the time, the original statement
                has been distorted.

POLTERGEIST PASSWORD

WALLY
Ohh, I think I like Baxstabber's rationale
better than yours, Zo. We're operating
under rules we thought were set in stone,
but that's because these instructions have
been passed down from someone who heard
them from a friend who heard them from a
friend who heard them from a
friend. . .just like Shelby said.

ALONZO
Jesus, fuck!

*Sounds of movement and unidentifiable
distortions.*

WALLY
What?

ALONZO
There was someone looking through the
window!

WALLY
There's no window in the studio, Zo.

ALONZO
I left the door open behind you,
motherfucker. I can see straight into the
kitchen. I looked at the window above the
sink and something was looking back at me,
and then it fuckin' disappeared.

*More squeaky chair movements and
distortions.*

SHELBY
I don't see anything.

                    WALLY
       I don't see anything either.

                   ALONZO
Of course you don't see anything! It's not
there now. I just said it disappeared.

                    WALLY
Okay, Zo. Calm down, brother. What did you
                think you saw?

                   ALONZO
I swear to God, Wally, if you keep acting
like I didn't see something when I say I
did I'm gonna beat you to death with your
              own microphone.

                   SHELBY
              What was it?

                   ALONZO
It was blurry. A face, but blurry.

                    WALLY
       Okay. . .can you be a bit more
    descriptive? What color was it?

                   ALONZO
It was pale white, man, but it looked like
it was twitching real bad or some shit.
Like shaking its head back and forth so
        fast that it was just a blur.

                    WALLY
Interesting. Wow, okay. Listeners, you
    heard his honest reaction there for
yourselves. Zombie Zo says he saw a white
blur of a face through my kitchen window.
  I should probably let you all know that
with this room being converted into a home

POLTERGEIST PASSWORD

studio, we always keep the door shut to soundproof it as best as we can. In fact, I can't think of a time when we've recorded when the door was open, but in the heat of the moment with the glass breaking a moment ago, the door didn't get shut. The door is behind me, over my right shoulder. Mr. Zombie Zo is seated beside me, and Shelby Baxstabber is on my other side. Zombie Zo is the only one of us with a partial view through the door. However, we do have a camera situated on the table directly in front of me, and I know for a fact that the entire wall behind me is in its frame, meaning it possibly caught what just happened.

ALONZO
Run that shit back. Right now. Come on.

SHELBY
I want to see it, too.

WALLY
Well, it seems a consensus has been reached, dear listeners. We will now review the footage for any sight of something out of the ordinary. Shelby, do you want to grab the camera?

SHELBY
Sure.

ALONZO
How do you even watch playback on that mini cam? Do you need to hook it up to your laptop or something?

The studio door slams shut. The audio distorts.

NICK ROBERTS

                    WALLY
                 Holy shit!

*Sounds of Wally's headphones hitting the
table and chairs squeaking.*

                   SHELBY
   The fucking door just slammed by itself.

                    WALLY
                  (off mic)
     Hey! Who the fuck is in my house?

                   ALONZO
            I didn't see anything.

                    WALLY
                  (off mic)
  None of us did. We were all looking at the
                   camera.

Something shatters against a hard surface.

                   SHELBY
                 Oh my God!

                   ALONZO
            Did you do that, Wally?

                    WALLY
                  (off mic)
  You think I'd throw my own camera against
                  the wall?

                   SHELBY
 Seriously, what the hell is going on? This
   doesn't feel right. I'm freaking out.

                   ALONZO
       Something is fucking with us.

POLTERGEIST PASSWORD

Sounds of Wally walking back to his seat and picking up his headphones.

WALLY
Do you guys have your phones on you?

SHELBY
Yes.

ALONZO
Right here.

WALLY
Turn on the cameras and let them record. I'm gonna do the same with mine. We have to capture what's happening.

SHELBY
I don't want to continue with this, Wally. Do you not feel that?

WALLY
Feel what?

SHELBY
The air. The temperature. It just feels. . .different.

WALLY
I, um, I do sense something off about the atmosphere now that you pointed it out.

ALONZO
It feels like we just walked into a damn cave or something.

SHELBY
I want to leave. We need to end this.

WALLY
Shelby, hold on now. I'm freaked out just
like you, but we can't leave.

ALONZO
And why the fuck not?

WALLY
No, it's not like that. We *can* leave. I
wasn't trying to imply anything like that.
I'm just saying this is why we created the
podcast, right?

ALONZO
You definitely spiked our damn drinks. You
sound fucking nuts right now.

WALLY
I didn't spike shit. Shelby, it's why we
started it, right?

SHELBY
Yeah.

WALLY
So, do you want to call 9-1-1 or go
running out of the house, or do you wanna
ride it out and make history?

ALONZO
Y'all have lost your damn minds.

SHELBY
Poltergeists don't kill people, Zo.

ALONZO
Huh?

SHELBY
In all the research I did for the show, I

POLTERGEIST PASSWORD

didn't encounter one case where a supposed poltergeist was blamed for a death.

WALLY
That's right. Remember the "angry child syndrome." They're just like kids who want attention.

ALONZO
Okay, y'all can play Ghostbusters all you want. I hope you catch some serious shit that's makes us all famous, but I'm getting the fuck out of here.

Sounds of Alonzo removing his headphones and dropping them on the table.

WALLY
Alonzo, wait!

SHELBY
Don't leave us, man. It's going to be wicked. We need you.

ALONZO
(off mic)
Sorry guys. I'm leaving.

The sound of the door opening.

ALONZO
What the—
(screams and grunts as he moves further away from the mic)

The door slams shut.

*Reporter's note: During this part of the broadcast, Alonzo is presumably pulled out of the studio as soon as the door is opened. Whether he opened it or not remains unknown. In a matter of three seconds, one can hear the sounds of his shoes across a hard floor and distant thuds like he is being dragged against his will. After doing research on Alonzo and visiting the house itself, it was discovered that he stood just over six feet tall and weighed approximately two hundred and twenty pounds. It would take an incredible force to move him from the studio to the top of the staircase in approximately three seconds. This part of the episode is one of the most debated topics as it provides a divisive stance for listeners. Either Alonzo was pulled by something with supernatural strength, or this was all audio effects for the elaborate hoax. This reporter is not so naïve to believe that sounds like that can't be created. Many audio experts have demonstrated in their own videos how simple it is to record a track that sounds exactly like this one. It would be, however, the first time *Broadcasts From the Grave* utilized any kind of audio theatrics if it was staged. According to interviews with family members, none of the three hosts possessed this skill set.

                    SHELBY
                   (screams)
              What was that?

                    WALLY
                  Alonzo!

Wally removes his headphones and lets them drop on the table.

                    WALLY
                   (off mic)
          I can't open the fucking door!

                    SHELBY
                 Pull on it!

                    WALLY
                   (off mic)
        What does it look like I'm doing?

POLTERGEIST PASSWORD

                    ALONZO
              (barely audible)
              Help!

                    SHELBY
          I'm calling the cops.

                    WALLY
                 (off mic)
              Do it.

A phone vibrates like it's ringing.

                    WALLY
                 (off mic)
              What's that?

The phone vibrates again.

                    WALLY
                 (off mic)
          Shelby! What's going on?

                    SHELBY
          Alonzo is calling me.

                    WALLY
                 (off mic)
     I don't see his phone in here. He's got it
              on him. Answer it!

                    SHELBY
     Hello? Wait what? I can barely hear you.

*Sounds of Wally moving across the room and
putting his headphones back on.*

                    WALLY
          Put it on speakerphone.

NICK ROBERTS

*A light thud of what is presumably the
cell phone being placed on the table.*

SHELBY
Alonzo, you're on speaker.

WALLY
(whispers)
Hold it up to the mic.

ALONZO
(whispers)
Guys? Can you hear me? Hello?

WALLY
Yeah, we can hear you. What the hell
happened? Are you okay?

ALONZO
(whispers)
Something pulled me up the stairs and
locked me in your room.

WALLY
What do you mean something? What was it?

ALONZO
(whispers)
It was that same goddamn thing I saw in
the window that I tried to tell you all
about, but you fuckin' blew it off, and
now I'm trapped in the goddamn closet
while that thing is out there somewhere.

SHELBY
Wait, you're in the closet?

ALONZO
(whispers)
Yeah. Call the cops right now. You don't

POLTERGEIST PASSWORD

want that thing coming in the studio. We
have to get out of here. This shit is for
real.

WALLY
Alonzo, you said it pulled you in my room.
How'd you get in my closet?

ALONZO
(whispers)
It threw me into the side of your bed, and
I crawled in here to hide. I don't know
where it is. Have you called the cops yet?

WALLY
Well, no. You're on Shelby's phone right
now, and I'm recording video with mine.

SHELBY
Are you fucking serious, Wally? Stop and
call 9-1-1. This has gone too far.

WALLY
Sorry, guys. I'm recording everything that
happens from here on out. Non-negotiable.

SHELBY
You are fucking unbelievable. Call the
cops or I quit the show.

WALLY
That's on you, Baxstabber.

SHELBY
Alonzo. I have to put you on hold so I can
call on my phone.

ALONZO
Do whatever. Just call them. I'm staying
on the line. I'm fucking terrified, Shelb.

SHELBY
It'll be okay. Hang on.

WALLY
Okay, listeners. Shelby has taken Alonzo
off speaker and switched over to dial out.

SHELBY
Fuck you, Wally!

WALLY
She just dialed 9-1-1. Keep it on
speakerphone.

*The phone rings three times, still on
speakerphone.*

OPERATOR
(female voice)
9-1-1, what is your emergency?

SHELBY
Hello, someone has broken into the house
we're in and has my friend trapped
upstairs. We're recording a—

OPERATOR
Okay, ma'am, calm down. What is your
address?

SHELBY
Wally, what's your house number?

WALLY
717

SHELBY
We're at 717 Tulane Road. Please hurry.

POLTERGEIST PASSWORD

OPERATOR
We don't need to hurry, ma'am. We're
already in the home.

SHELBY
What?

OPERATOR
We're already in your home. You called us
earlier.

WALLY
Excuse me? Lady, is this a joke?

OPERATOR
(the female voice gradually turns back
into Alonzo's)
This is not a joke. Your friend is dead.
There's no need to rush. No need to run.
Not anymore.
(Alonzo laughs)

WALLY
Switch back over to Alonzo's line.

*A loud burst of hissing static distorts the
audio.*

WALLY
Fuck! Was that your phone?

SHELBY
Yeah. It's dead. The screen won't even
turn on. What the fuck? What the fuck was
that, Wally? Did you hear her voice? She
turned into Alonzo!

WALLY
I heard. I, uh, I don't know what to say.

                    SHELBY
            Use your phone to call.

                    WALLY
            Yeah, okay. Fine.

Faint thuds can be heard in the distance.

                    WALLY
            Wait. Do you hear that?

*The thuds get louder like someone is coming
down the staircase.*

                    SHELBY
            Yeah.

                    WALLY
            He's coming back downstairs.

Someone pounds on the door three times.

                    SHELBY
            Jesus!

*A loud thud like a door being flung open
and hitting the wall.*

                    WALLY
            What the fuck?

*Distorted sounds as both hosts remove their
headphones and drop them on the table.
Glass shatters like lightbulbs exploding.*

                    WALLY
                  (off mic)
            Get to the corner.

POLTERGEIST PASSWORD

SHELBY
(off mic)
What is that? What the fuck is that?

WALLY
(off mic)
I don't know. I can't see shit. The damn
lights exploded.

SHELBY
(off mic, whispers)
Over there! Someone's standing in the
doorway.

WALLY
(off mic)
Alonzo? Is that you?

UNKNOWN
(off mic)
Alonzo is dead.

WALLY
(off mic)
What's going on? Who are you?

UNKNOWN
(off mic)
You don't know?

SHELBY
(off mic)
Oh my God. It's floating.

WALLY
(off mic)
Shh. Look, we're sorry for what we did.

NICK ROBERTS

UNKNOWN
(off mic)
(distorted, screeching wail)

A commotion like chairs being knocked over, bodies hitting the walls.

SHELBY
(off mic)
Wally!

WALLY
(off mic)
Let her go!

Shelby's screams are loud and close to the mic and then move further away. The door slams shut.

SHELBY
(off mic)
Wally! No! Please!

Distant thuds similar to when Alonzo was dragged up the staircase.

WALLY
(off mic)
Shelby!

Footsteps hurry across the room and the doorknob is jiggled.

WALLY
(off mic)
Fuck! Open the door! Let me out of here!

A door in the distance (presumably upstairs) slams shut. There are loud pounds like Wally is hitting the studio door.

POLTERGEIST PASSWORD

                    WALLY
                  (off mic)
Shelby! I'm sorry. Do you hear me? I'm so—

*A hissing pop of static cuts Wally off, and
all is quiet.*

                    WALLY
                  (off mic)
                What the hell?

*Twenty-seven seconds of relative silence
pass before the sound of the headphones
being picked up from the table and put on
can be heard.*

                    WALLY
                (whispering)
Hello. I don't know what to say or how to
  explain what's happened, but there needs
to be some kind of record, so no one tries
   what we did tonight. The light in the
studio exploded minutes ago when whatever
   that thing was opened the door. There's
 glass all over the table in front of me.
I'm sitting in Shelby's seat so I can see
  the door. Somehow, the light in the room
   is back on. There's a new bulb in there
 because there's still fucking glass from
the old one everywhere. But when that door
   opened, Shelby and I moved to the far
corner of the room. We saw this thing that
  looked like a person but not really. It
was like shadowy, and it didn't have feet
  that were touching the floor. I know the
power in the house didn't completely shut
   off because I could see light from the
other part of the house behind the thing.
  I don't know if the mics picked up what
  happened, but I tried to talk to it. It

made the loudest fucking scream and literally flew across the studio and grabbed Shelby. She knocked me against the wall when it dragged her out. It pulled her across the table and into the hallway in seconds, like she didn't weigh a pound. The door slammed shut by itself, and the thing took her upstairs where I'm guessing it took Alonzo. As of right now, I don't know if either one of them are alive. I don't hear anything coming from the other side of the door. I don't know what this thing or these things want. This is not a hoax. It's not part of the show. I'm fucking terrified for my life right now. If you're listening to this and we're all dead, do not do the Polter—

A phone buzzes.

WALLY
Fuck!

Sounds of Wally picking up the phone from the table.

WALLY
Jesus Christ. Okay, it says Shelby is calling me right now. Shelby's phone is on the table in front of me.
(sighs)
Fuck it. Hello?

Distorted white noise hisses through the audio. Wally presumably puts the phone on speaker mode.

UNKNOWN CHILD'S VOICE
(speakerphone)
Can you see me?

POLTERGEIST PASSWORD

Five seconds of silence.

WALLY
No. I'm in an empty room. What have you—

UNKNOWN CHILD'S VOICE
(off mic)
Down here.

WALLY
Oh, my fucking God! What the fuck? There's
a fucking dead kid under the table!

UNKNOWN CHILD'S VOICE
(laughter)

WALLY
I can't move my legs. I can't fucking move
my legs.

*The doorknob jiggles, and the door slams
against the wall.*

WALLY
Ouch! Fuck! The fucking thing bit me.
It's. . .it's just fucking biting my leg
and staring at me. Dear God, help me.
(crying)
I can't do this. I'm not looking. I can't
do this. Please make it go away. Make it
go away. This is a dream. That drop was
spiked with something, and I'm just
tripping balls right now.

*There's a scurrying sound as the child's
laughter fades away.*

WALLY
(hyperventilating)
Oh, Jesus. What the fuck was that? It's

gone. The door's open, but it's dark out there now. The studio light is still on, but I can't see shit out there. I swear there was a fucking dead kid gnawing on my leg just now.

UNKNOWN VOICES
(speaking in unison off mic)
You called us. This is what you wanted, right? For your show?

WALLY
(whispers)
Jesus Christ, they're in the hallway but I can't see them.

UNKNOWN
We're behind you, too.

WALLY
(crying)
They're in the room, but I can't turn around. I can't move. It's like something is holding me down, but I can't see it.

UNKNOWN
Is this better?

WALLY
(screams hysterically)

UNKNOWN
(laughs)

WALLY
(crying)
Oh my God! Oh my God! Get off me! Get off me! What the fuck? I'm sorry! I'm so sorry! I've learned my lesson! I promise! Just don't kill me.

POLTERGEIST PASSWORD

UNKNOWN
Look at me, coward.

WALLY
(crying)
I don't want to.

The sound of glass being moved around on the table.

UNKNOWN
Look at me or I'll cut off your eyelids
with a lightbulb.

WALLY
No! No! No! Okay, okay. I'll look.

Ten seconds pass, and the only sound detected is Wally's frantic breathing.

UNKNOWN
What's the matter, Wally? Do we frighten
you?

WALLY
(crying)
I didn't mean for this to happen. If I can
reverse it, I will. Just tell me how.

Distorted audio as multiple entities erupt in a fit of laughter.

WALLY
Stop! Stop! Please. I'll do anything.

More distorted laughter.

ALONZO
There is one thing you can do to help us,
Wally.

WALLY
Zo? Jesus Christ, what did they do to you?
How did you two get in here? Why are you
wearing your headphones?

SHELBY
Do you want to help us, Wally?

WALLY
How are you here right now? Oh my God.
What did they do to your eyes?

ALONZO
You brought us the Poltergeist Password.
You killed us.

SHELBY
We know what it's like to be dead now.

WALLY
(crying)
I'm so sorry.

ALONZO
It's peaceful, Wally. It really is.

SHELBY
It's like you're floating down a warm
stream and every part of you tingles with
joy.

ALONZO
There's no pain. No fear. Just eternal
bliss.

Loud distorted hissing.

UNKNOWN
Until they take it all away from you!

POLTERGEIST PASSWORD

WALLY
Oh fuck!

UNKNOWN
We're sucked back into a place we don't
belong because of your stupid fucking
games!

WALLY
Zo! Shelby! No, don't do that!

Repeated wet, piercing sounds.

WALLY
I'm going to fucking throw up. Stop! Oh,
Jesus Christ.

ALONZO
We don't need our skin, Wally. The pain of
peeling it off like this is nothing
compared to how it feels to be pulled back
into this world.

SHELBY
Here, Wally. Hold this.

Sounds of Wally vomiting.

SHELBY
Oh, don't be such a baby. It's just my
face. Put it on.

WALLY
(coughs and spits)
I'm not putting your fucking face on. Get
that shit away from me.

UNKNOWN VOICES
Put it on!

                    WALLY
                  (sobbing)
Okay. Okay. Oh my God, this is fucking
                 disgusting.

                   ALONZO
What does it feel like, Wally?

                   SHELBY
Yeah, tell the listeners.

                    WALLY
It's wet. . .and sticky. It feels like a
        rotten Halloween mask.

                   ALONZO
Go ahead. Put it on your face.

                    WALLY
I'm going to be fucking sick again.

                   SHELBY
Here, I'll help you.

                    WALLY
No! Stay away from me!

*There are sounds of a struggle. Wally
grunts and screams like he's fighting
something off. The screaming and piercing
sounds go on for one minute and thirteen
seconds.*

                   SHELBY
There. All done.

                    WALLY
              (muffled cries)
Please. Take it off.

POLTERGEIST PASSWORD

ALONZO
But you're just now starting to feel our
pain, Wally. Tell the listeners all about
it. Tell them so they know what will
happen to them if they play Poltergeist
Password.

WALLY
(muffled)
I can't move. My body is paralyzed. It's
hard to talk. They used the glass from the
lightbulb to. . .(crying). . .to attach
Shelby's face to mine. It hurts so fucking
bad.

SHELBY
You don't know what pain is, but you will,
Wally. Alonzo, me, you, we're all fucked.
Just like our words said at the beginning
of the game. You wanna know why?

WALLY
(muffled moan)
No.

ALONZO
We're all fucked because the next time
someone plays the game, we're the ones who
have to go. We're the ones who have our
flesh ripped from our celestial bodies to
be rendered corporeal again, torn off,
layer by layer. (laughs.) You did that to
us, Wally!

WALLY
(muffled)
I'm sorry. I'm sorry.

SHELBY
It's too late for all that, Wally. It's
your turn now.

WALLY
(muffled)
My turn for what?

UNKNOWN
To change.

WALLY
(muffled)
No!

Wally gasps. Headphones bang off the table. Static distorts the sound of Wally's fading screams. The same thuds are heard as if he's being dragged up the stairs like Alonzo and Shelby had been. A door slams upstairs, and Wally's faint screams abruptly end.

Two minutes and six seconds pass. The only sounds during this time are the occasional squeak of a studio chair or distorted bursts of static.

There are banging sounds like silverware being thrown across the kitchen. Cabinets and doors open and slam. Multiple light bulbs explode one after another at different volumes, presumably coming from different areas of the house. Furniture grinds across floors and tips over with loud thuds.

Faint, childlike laughter can be heard way off mic, and then the feed goes silent for two minutes and six seconds again.

POLTERGEIST PASSWORD

Heavy footsteps gradually descend the staircase and enter the studio. A chair is pulled out and someone sits down in the squeaky seat. Labored breathing can be heard off mic. There's a ruffling as headphones are picked up from the table and put on.

A voice that sounds like an imitation of Wally begins to speak.

WALLY(?)
Hello, dear listener, it's your old pal, Weird Wally, here. I'm joined by my cohosts Mr. Zombie Zo and Shelby Baxstabber in the studio as we bid our final goodbyes, for this is indeed our farewell episode. But before we sign off, Ms. Baxstabber, how about a message from our sponsors?

SHELBY(?)
Sure, Wally. We'd like to thank Spooky Socks for the years of support. From day one, they've enabled us to record *Broadcasts From the Grave* for you. Don't let the fact that we're dead dissuade you from owning the coolest socks on the market. Even though we won't need socks in the Hell we're about to endure, we still want you to have not only the most frightening footwear around but the most comfortable. Back to you, Wally.

WALLY(?)
Thanks, Ms. Baxstabber. Mr. Zombie Zo, as always, we await your final verdict on the case presented in this episode. What's your official ruling on Poltergeist Password?

NICK ROBERTS

                    ALONZO(?)
               Don't fucking play it.

                     WALLY(?)
      Cutting straight to the chase as always.
      That's why we love you. Okay then. I think
      we're out of time here. Once again, thanks
         to all the listeners who've been with us
            over the years, and I just want to
             reiterate that unless you want your
         fucking flesh peeled off, stay away from
                 Poltergeist Password.

*The show's spooky theme song begins to play
and slowly fades out.*

*Static and screams of agony distort the
audio and cuts off.*

                  END OF TRANSCRIPT

                        ***

As previously stated at the beginning of this report, the missing
persons cases for Wally Miller, Alonzo Lawrence, and Shelby
Baxter remain open. Whether you believe this to be a hoax, a prank
gone awry by unknown hallucinogens, or a legitimate encounter
with something beyond the laws of science and rational
explanation, is your choice. But it is the hope of this reporter that
someone reads this and comes forward with any evidence that
leads to further understanding of what truly transpired during the
final episode of *Broadcasts From the Grave*. If you know anything
about the legend of the Poltergeist Password or the whereabouts
of the missing persons, please contact the proper authorities.

Until then, this mystery remains unsolved.

THE END

THE END?

Not if you want to dive into more of the Dark Tide series.

Check out our amazing website and online store
or download our latest catalog here.
https://geni.us/CLPCatalog

We always have great new projects and content on the website to dive into, as well as a newsletter, behind the scenes options, social media platforms, our own dark fiction shared-world series and our very own webstore. Our webstore even has categories specifically for KU books, non-fiction, anthologies, and of course more novels and novellas.

ABOUT THE AUTHORS

Leigh was born and raised in the garden county of Wicklow, Ireland. She lives by the Irish Sea with the love of her life, two wonderful boys, a black Labrador, and a three-legged cat that hates people. She describes herself as being both feral and aggressively friendly and apologises in advance for swearing in front of your children. You can find out more about Leigh's work and any upcoming releases on social media at LeighKennyWrites.

Dan Franklin wrote his first attempt at a horror novel when he was seven. It was terrible. He has, since, improved. The Amazon best selling author of *These Things Linger, Down Into the Sea,* and *The Eater of Gods*, Dan Franklin lives in Maryland with his extremely understanding wife, his cosmically radiant children, and a socially crippling obsession with things that creep. He can be contacted through social media (Facebook.com/DanFranklinAuthor) or at DanFranklinAuthor.com

Nick Roberts is a native West Virginian and a doctoral graduate of Marshall University. He is an active member of the Horror Writers Association and the Horror Authors Guild. His works include Anathema, The Exorcist's House, It Haunts the Mind & Other Stories, Mean Spirited, and others. He currently resides in South Carolina with his family and is an advocate for people in recovery from substance use disorder.

Readers . . .

Thank you for reading *Urban Legends*. We hope you enjoyed this 20th book in our Dark Tide series.

If you have a moment, please review *Urban Legends* at the store where you bought it.

Help other readers by telling them why you enjoyed this book. No need to write an in-depth discussion. Even a single sentence will be greatly appreciated. Reviews go a long way to helping a book sell, and is great for an author's career. It'll also help us to continue publishing quality books.

Thank you again for taking the time to journey with Crystal Lake Publishing.

Visit our Linktree page for a list of our social media platforms. https://linktr.ee/CrystalLakePublishing

Follow us on Amazon:

your world, doors within your mind, from talented authors who sacrifice so much for a moment of your time.

There are some amazing small presses out there, and through collaboration and open forums we will continue to support other presses in the goal of helping authors and showing the world what quality small presses are capable of accomplishing. No one wins when a small press goes down, so we will always be there to support hardworking, legitimate presses and their authors. We don't see Crystal Lake as the best press out there, but we will always strive to be the best, strive to be the most interactive and grateful, and even blessed press around. No matter what happens over time, we will also take our mission very seriously while appreciating where we are and enjoying the journey.

What do we offer our authors that they can't do for themselves through self-publishing?

We are big supporters of self-publishing (especially hybrid publishing), if done with care, patience, and planning. However, not every author has the time or inclination to do market research, advertise, and set up book launch strategies. Although a lot of authors are successful in doing it all, strong small presses will always be there for the authors who just want to do what they do best: write.

What we offer is experience, industry knowledge, contacts and trust built up over years. And due to our strong brand and trusting fanbase, every Crystal Lake Publishing book comes with weight of respect. In time our fans begin to trust our judgment and will try a new author purely based on our support of said author.

With each launch we strive to fine-tune our approach, learn from our mistakes, and increase our reach. We continue to assure our authors that we're here for them and that we'll carry the weight of the launch and dealing with third parties while they focus on their strengths—be it writing, interviews, blogs, signings, etc.

We also offer several mentoring packages to authors that include knowledge and skills they can use in both traditional and self-publishing endeavours.

We look forward to launching many new careers.

This is what we believe in. What we stand for. This will be our legacy.

Welcome to Crystal Lake Publishing—
Where stories come alive!

www.ingramcontent.com/pod-product-compliance
Lightning Source LLC
Chambersburg PA
CBHW060322310726
48976CB00007B/2404